FIGHTING THE FIRE

A WARRIOR FIGHT CLUB NOVEL

LAURA KAYE

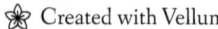

READ HARD WITH LAURA KAYE

Hard Ink Series
HARD AS IT GETS
HARD AS YOU CAN
HARD TO HOLD ON TO
HARD TO COME BY
HARD TO BE GOOD
HARD TO LET GO
HARD AS STEEL
HARD EVER AFTER
HARD TO SERVE

Hearts in Darkness Duet
HEARTS IN DARKNESS
LOVE IN THE LIGHT

Heroes Series
HER FORBIDDEN HERO
ONE NIGHT WITH A HERO

Stand Alone Titles
DARE TO RESIST
JUST GOTTA SAY

THE WARRIOR FIGHT CLUB SERIES

This fight club has one rule:
You must be a veteran…

FIGHTING FOR EVERYTHING
FIGHTING FOR WHAT'S HIS
WORTH FIGHTING FOR
FIGHTING THE FIRE

To all of you, for hanging in there with me

CHAPTER ONE

DANIELA ENGLAND WAS raring for a fight.

The day felt like it'd been a whole week long already and it was only four o'clock in the afternoon. To begin with, she'd been part of a team that hadn't been able to resuscitate a stroke patient. Then she'd had another patient leave against medical advice. And the cherry on top had been getting harangued by the Emergency Department director for maybe the dozenth time to accept the open designated charge nurse position on the 7AM – 7PM shift. Which, no way. He kept pitching it as a promotion, but it came with massive headaches for only another $1.50 per hour, so Dani had been saying no for weeks.

She loved being a nurse and adored knowing that her words and actions had the power to put her patients at ease, but dear God sometimes the losses and red tape threatened to suck the life blood right out of her soul.

All of which meant she was more than ready for Warrior Fight Club.

She walked into the big gym space at Full Contact where WFC met every Saturday and immediately bit back a curse. Because her gaze scanned for one particular club member. Sean

Riddick. Which was freaking ridiculous since he drove her crazy.

And not in a good way.

Well, *mostly* not in a good way.

Annnd that thought proved she needed to beat on some things. Repeatedly. Because Sean was arrogant, sarcastic, immature, an adrenaline junkie, and a player. In other words, he was irritating in the extreme.

If only he weren't *also* hot as fuck. *And* a hot fuck. Really, they were interchangeable truths.

Girl, *what is the matter with you? You already made that mistake once.*

That was the tenor of Dani's thoughts as she crossed to the bleachers where the others had dropped their bags. She caught Tara Hunter's eye and waved to the former navy diver who jogged over as Dani looked for her gloves.

"Hey," Tara said, her long brown waves pulled back in a messy bun—one that left the curved scar running down the pale pink skin of Tara's throat fully exposed. The diving accident that caused it had led to her medical discharge from the military —yet she was still working in commercial diving, just like Dani still worked as a nurse. Maybe that was why, despite Tara being a relative WFC newbie compared to Dani's almost five years, they'd clicked right away.

"Hey," Dani said, eyeballing her friend. "You're beaming. What's up with that?"

Tara flushed. "Nothing's up. Things are just good right now."

Smirking, Dani teased her. "And by 'things' do you by any chance mean the hot bomb squad cop you're shacking up with?"

Laughter spilled out of the younger woman as she elbowed Dani in the arm. "I might in fact mean the hot bomb squad cop I'm shacking up with. Yes."

"Mmhmm. I thought so," Dani said, genuinely happy for her friend. It hadn't been that many months ago that Tara had confided that things hadn't worked out between her and Jesse Anderson—one of WFC's newest members and the hot cop in question—so seeing them so happily together now was really nice. Every once in a while, good things happened to good people, and that was always the best. Dani wasn't sure why that thought weighed on her shoulders so heavily, but it kinda did.

You know exactly why, Dani. She heaved a breath.

"Hey, you okay?"

"What? Why?" Dani said, brazening it out.

Giving her a long, too-appraising look, Tara shrugged. "You just seem like you have the weight of the world on your shoulders."

Directness was one of the things Dani liked about Tara, so she gave her at least part of the truth. "Just a hard shift at work. Comes with the territory."

"Maybe beating the crap out of something will help," Tara said with an understanding smile.

"Exactly. Or *someone*." She grinned.

Tara laughed, but her gaze shifted to a point just beyond Dani, which was all the notice she had before a voice rumbled low and dangerous in her ear.

"Got anyone in mind, Daniela?"

Sean said her name as if his tongue caressed every letter, and she cursed the shiver that raced up her spine—the shiver that resulted from knowing *exactly* how damn good his tongue felt. She turned slowly, lazily, as if she were bored to tears. No way was she letting him know he got to her. So she gave him a once-over that she hoped read as full of disdain.

Even though, damn. *DAMN.*

So tall she had to tilt her head back to roll her eyes at him. Dark hair cut short because it curled when he let it get even a little length to it. With scars near his eye and hairline and a nose that had been broken, his face was too beat up to be handsome. But it was even more interesting for having character—of the fearless   *I-run-into-burning-buildings-to-save-people-and-some-times-get-hurt-doing-it* variety. And then there were the tattoos —on his neck, shoulders, arms, the back of one hand, not to mention the hard muscles underneath, because of course the guy was freaking cut, with shoulders like mountains and thighs like tree trunks. Sean oozed unquestionable strength and a fierce masculinity.

He knew he looked good.

He wasn't wrong. Damn him.

And damn *her* for being stupid enough to find out just how good he was. Just once, eight months ago, at that fucking Halloween party with the yummy-but-evil Jell-O shooters and him in that should've-been-ridiculous-but-was-insanely-hot gladiator costume. The one that had put his impressive shoulders, chest, and thighs on display. And since he'd been injured earlier that week in a fire, he'd come complete with a healing head laceration and giant bruise on his upper back that made his costume feel even more authentic. So, yeah, she'd given into his appeal just that once.

But it'd been enough to keep her body attuned to him even as her head screamed *been there, done that, shouldn't have done it the first time and ain't doing it again.*

Dani sniffed. "Not you."

His grin was pure wicked sin. "You sure about that?"

She sighed. "Absolutely."

He gave a low chuckle. "Well, you're welcome to *try* to beat the shit out of me any time."

"Don't you have anyone else to irritate?"

"Oh, I irritate you, do I?" he asked, dropping his bag to the floor. He winked at Tara. "Hey, T."

"Hey, Sean," she said, amusement plain in her voice.

But Dani was too busy noticing that more people had filled in during the few minutes since she'd arrived to dignify his attempts to goad her with a response. Billy Parrish, Noah Cortez, and Moses Griffin were talking over by the water fountain, and Coach Mack was rolling out a cart of gear with the help of Leo Hawkins and Colby Richmond, two of the original members from when the club had first formed eight years before. All prior military, of course, since being a veteran was the first rule here. It was the one place in Daniela's life where she remained connected with her old life and career in the army.

Just then, one of the few other women who belonged to WFC walked through the door. "Oh, Jayne's here," Dani said, surprised because her friend hadn't attended in weeks.

Without another word to Sean, Dani and Tara left him to greet her.

Halfway across the gym, Tara leaned close. "Seriously, do you really dislike Riddick or are the two of you in a perpetual state of foreplay?"

Dani threw her a look that made the other woman chuckle. "Ugh, not you, too," she said, remembering the awkward dinner where Jesse had asked in front of everyone how long Dani and Sean had been together. Apparently others could sense the weird chemistry that tried to tie the two of them together, even though the last thing Dani wanted was being tied to, well, anyone—let alone Riddick. "You really can't tell?"

Tara twisted her lips and shook her head. "Nope. But something's different between you guys lately, and I'm dying to know the story."

"There's no story," Dani said. Probably too fast. Definitely too fast, given that Tara had also picked up on the heightened friction between them. Because, of course, there was a *big* freaking story.

So. Big.

Dani at least had to give Sean credit for honoring his word and keeping their one night a secret.

"Suuuure." Tara arched an eyebrow, and Dani thanked God that they'd reached Jayne.

Jayne Harper was petite and curvy with warm brown skin and pretty shoulder-length black curls. "So glad you could make it," Dani said, happy to see the former Marine who was also the sole caregiver for her elderly father and couldn't always get away on Saturdays for WFC.

They hugged. "I've been dying to get back, but Dad's appointments lately have taken over our whole lives."

"How's he doing?" Dani asked as something inside her chest squeezed just a little. It had been her own father's death when she was just eight had been a big part of what made her want to pursue a career in medicine.

"Actually, he's been doing pretty good lately," Jayne said with a smile. "Warmer weather always helps his arthritis and lifts his spirits."

"Oh good. I'm happy to hear it and to get to see you," Dani said. "You remember Tara?"

"Yeah, of course." Jayne extended her hand for a shake.

Tara returned it. "I wouldn't blame you if you didn't. I'm good with faces but terrible with names."

Jayne laughed. "No worries. I have the memory of an elephant but I'm not always sure that remembering everything is the best either."

Coach Mack blew a whistle and clapped his hands. "Take your places and let's get started everyone."

They spread out on the floor. As restless and unsettled as Dani felt, WFC was exactly what she needed. She breathed through the stretches and yoga positions they did at the start of every club meeting. Because WFC was as much about training the *mind* as it was about training the body.

Problem was, this time of year her mind fought tooth and nail to pull her in directions she didn't want to go. She never did well come July.

Dani might not have been in the army anymore, but with nursing she still did similar work—work filled with its own losses and stress, and work that so often reminded her of people she'd lost years ago. Back when her patients were frequently people she'd been stationed or trained with at Bagram Air Base in Afghanistan. Back when she'd loved little more than her work as a nurse doing combat medical evacuations on Black Hawks.

Until her army husband had died while she'd been on one of her flight shifts. And it'd been hours before she'd found out Anthony was gone.

She and Anthony had met as ROTC members in college. From the very start, they'd accepted and even prized that they were both planning military careers. But as supportive as Anthony had been, her training to become certified to do aeromedical critical care evacuation and transport had been one of their biggest fights. He'd thought it too dangerous. Too unnecessarily risky when everything they did on deployment was already risky enough. But she'd been stubborn. She could still hear her granny encouraging her to look for the helpers when bad things happened, so Dani had always wanted to be a helper. And, more than that, she wanted to be forward deployed. On the front lines. Being one of the people who made a difference between life and death in the moment when it mattered most. Anthony had finally come around to supporting her, and then she hadn't been there for him when it was his time.

"Okay," Coach Mack said. "Pair up. Puncher versus kicker drills. Five-minute rounds."

Back at the bleachers, Dani pulled on her padded black fingerless gloves and shin guards. She returned to the floor to find Tara and Jayne pairing up, then turned again to find Sean grinning and holding out his hands in invitation. She almost groaned. But fine, whatever. She could handle Sean. Maybe his annoyingly hot...*everything* would even fuel the fire in her belly.

The fire of loss. Of grief. Of anger.

Not that it ever really went out. Because, in the end, her love of her work had kept her from being there when her husband had needed her most.

Kept her from even saying good-bye. And they'd thought deploying through the married army couple program would give them *more* time together...

"Punch or kick?" Sean asked. "Lady's choice."

She rolled her eyes. "I'm no fucking lady."

He smirked and looked like he had so many things he wanted to say. But, for once, he kept his sarcasm to himself.

"I'll take punching," Dani said, ready as hell to land her first hit. Ready for fighting to focus her to the point where it was all she could think about.

And she didn't have to wonder why she needed that so much. The sixth anniversary of Anthony's death was less than two weeks away. July 3rd. And she couldn't avoid thinking about Anthony, and about how she'd failed him.

Or about her father, and how he'd died in a construction accident when she was eight.

Or about the mama she'd never known, who'd gotten an infection during labor that killed her when Dani had only been two weeks old.

Or about her granny, her mother's mother, who'd struggled all her life with diabetes and died when Dani was fifteen.

Or about her nana and pap, her dad's parents who'd raised her after he died, and how they were gone now, too.

In the end, everyone always left her. Without always under-standing why, she'd survived each and every loss. And the anniversary of Anthony's death was the strongest reminder that being alone was apparently her lot in life.

Hopefully, the next two hours would at least help take her mind off of it.

"Bring it," Sean said, giving her a wink.

Ignoring his head games, Dani got into position. Fists up, elbows close to her ribs, lead leg forward. In this drill, Sean as the kicker could only make offensive moves with his legs. While, as the puncher, she couldn't use her legs at all. Which meant she had to get in close while defending against his kicks.

They circled. Feinted. Attacked.

Sean was strong as hell, but she was faster by a lot. Dani used that to her advantage. Blocking and dodging his kicks and then getting inside to attack his ribs and gut and kidneys in the spare seconds before he regained his footing.

Each punch she landed released a pressure valve some-where deep in her brain. And that release was so fundamental that she barely felt the kicks that Sean landed. Not that she gave him much chance to get them in, because she kept him close, under pressure, and on the defense blocking her punches.

"Damn, woman," he said, respect and wariness plain in his voice.

"You told me to bring it," she said, looking for another in. He blocked a shot at his ribs and delivered a spinning side kick that landed on the side of her thigh.

"Someone has some aggression to work out today," he said.

"Do you have to talk so much?" she asked, sweat curling down the side of her face as she attacked again. This time she drove forward, forcing him to retreat and not letting him get in a kick.

Sean blocked and covered and dodged until they were in a

clinch, breathing hard and face to face with no room to punch or kick. And for no good reason, heat *roared* over Dani. Heat that almost incinerated her from the inside out. Maybe it was the bulk of his muscles or the slick slide of their sweat or his scent of clean soap from a recent shower that couldn't quite remove the hint of fire from his skin and hair.

As if he sensed it, Sean's dark eyes flashed hot and his jaw went tight. Breaking the rules, he grabbed her around the waist and pulled her in close, letting her feel his erection for one spare moment before taking her to the mats in a controlled move that showed just how freaking strong he was. She expected to get the wind knocked out of her, but he'd more laid her out than knocked her down.

A whistle blew. "Switch up," Colby called. "And follow the damn rules, Riddick. We're not doing ground work right now."

Everyone laughed.

But Dani and Sean were caught in a staring contest with their faces mere inches apart.

She wanted him inside her so bad that she nearly gave voice to it.

Her brain went immediately to *that night*.

How they'd circled each other throughout that whole damn party. How Sean had walked her to her car, parked right in front of his, which she'd begrudgingly thought sweet despite her insistence she didn't need a damn chaperone. How they'd started bantering about *something* she couldn't even remember now—because all she could remember was how desperately aroused she'd felt. How she'd teasingly punched him and he'd caught her arm and hauled her in against him. How the shock of his erection against her hip had made her look up at him. And how he'd claimed her mouth and she'd let him.

Oh, hell yeah, she'd let him do that and so much more...

And she wanted it again.

It was that thought that finally made her brain come back online. "Get. Off."

His brow arched. Just the tiniest bit. "You can take your aggression out on me anytime." He spoke in a rushed whisper, but the words impacted her like a body slam, pressing her back into the floor with some unseen force. Because she'd heard that tone in his voice before, when she'd straddled his lap on the big bench of his pick-up and finally taken him deep.

"Fucking hell, Dani. Take all of me."

"Now," Dani said, hoping he didn't hear that her voice was affected, too.

In a move that seemed too lithe for someone his size, Sean hopped up then extended his hand to her.

Shook as she was, Dani accepted his help, then regretted it when he didn't immediately release her hand but instead held her right in front of him—exactly like he had that night. "Just say the word."

Dani swallowed hard. "Hold your breath waiting for it. *Please.*" She glared up at him, irritated with herself for letting him see inside her for that one unguarded moment when her body had reacted so viscerally to his. It was like that night had tuned their bodies into the same wavelength, and now they could communicate whether she wanted it or not.

Amusement and challenge slid into his gaze. "You'll not only say it, Dani. You'll beg me for it."

She barked out a laugh, that was how incredulously funny she found his little pronouncement. What a giant, arrogant asshole. "Oh. *Definitely* hold your breath for that, Riddick. You'll be a box full of dust before that *ever* happens."

Sean looked at her with a knowing gaze. A gaze that told her he remembered too freaking much about that night, too. She might've punched that annoyingly sexy arrogance off his face if headshots hadn't been off limits at WFC.

Instead, Dani tugged her hand free. "Are you going to spar with me or did you want to braid my fucking hair while you keep talking?"

He knocked his gloves together and scanned his gaze around her face to where the length of her French braid trailed over her shoulder. "Looks like you already took care of your hair, sweetheart. So let's spar. My turn to punch." His grin was so annoyingly satisfied. He knew he'd gotten to her.

Dani rolled her eyes. "You're still talking," she said launching a round house kick at him. And then it was on again. The fighting. The focus. The fire deep in her belly.

But, damnit, the heat was still there, too.

The kind of soul-deep, bone-melting heat she'd only ever felt with one other man, one who'd died six years before.

And Dani freaking hated Sean Riddick for that. For making her body want something her head and her heart weren't about to allow her to have. Not again. Because she didn't want a relationship, a man in her life, or a frenemies-with-benefits situation, and certainly not any of those with a man who drove her freaking batty ninety percent of the time and made her worry about him the other ten because he raced into every burning building he could. That was all way more aggravation than any woman needed.

Nope. She'd done the whole relationship thing with a hotheaded warrior and ended up a widow at the age of twenty-eight, thank you very much. So the last thing she needed was to set herself up to be left again.

Sean landed a kidney punch that stole Dani's breath. *Because you're thinking about him and relationships and Anthony and not fucking focusing. Damnit.*

"Shit, Daniela. You okay?" Sean asked, his face blanched, his expression full of regret.

She forced a deep breath but reveled in the pain. Little

made it easier to focus than pain. "It was a perfectly fair hit, Sean. I'm fine." Her voice didn't sound quite right even to herself.

"I'm sorry," he said, shoulders down, hands slack at his sides.

The last thing she wanted was sympathy. That reminded her too much of the way people had treated her right after she'd learned that IEDs had taken out a third of Anthony's convoy. "Let's go already."

"Dani, just take a minute—"

"Sean, I'm fine," she snapped. Of course, she did it in a way that made it clear she wasn't fine. But whatever. She could handle hot Sean Riddick being an asshole, but not hot Sean Riddick being a good guy. The hot good guy was a whole helluva lot harder to resist.

"Yeah, okay," he said, not at all sounding convinced. Which probably explained why he backed off on the power of his punches after that. And that just pissed her off even more.

"Stop holding back," she finally bit out. Because he wasn't blocking as aggressively anymore either.

He ignored her. His punches felt more like taps.

Dani inhaled to tell him exactly what she thought of that when the whistle blew again, marking the end of the drill. She arched a brow at him and silently told him everything she thought about his treating her with kid gloves. He arched a brow right back telling her what he thought of her *I'm fine* routine.

"Fine," she bit out.

"Fine," he retorted.

Coach Mack gave them their next drill instructions, which fortunately didn't involve partners this time.

But before she and Sean parted ways, she turned to him. "You know what? Next time treat me like I'm your equal in here, okay?"

Sean's whole face slid into a frown and something she

couldn't read roiled behind those dark eyes. "Fuck that, Dani. You think I wouldn't go easy on anyone I just hurt? I more than see you as an equal. Hell, I think you're a lot fuckin' better than me." With that, he walked away.

Well. She blinked. Fuck.

"Everything okay?" a deep voice said from beside her.

And Dani...literally had no idea. She wasn't sure which had her more gobsmacked—the flash of hurt she would've sworn she saw in Sean's gaze, the guilt and regret she heard in his voice, or that he thought she was better than him.

"Dani?"

She turned to Moses, a former Army Ranger and another mountain of a man who'd joined WFC at about the same time Dani had. "Yeah, everything's fine." There was that word again. It wasn't true this time either. Because now she felt bad about being bitchy toward Sean when he'd just been looking out for her. Apparently. Damnit. "Thanks, Mo."

Tara was right. Things had gotten more intense between them since the night they'd shared. And Dani wasn't sure what to do about that. It wasn't like she could avoid the man altogether. Not when they both belonged to WFC, and not when Sean's work sometimes brought him to Dani's emergency department.

Mo nodded and ran a towel over the deep brown of his face and bald head. "You coming out afterwards?"

"Uh, yeah, I think so," she said. A group of them usually went out to dinner after WFC, and Dani often joined. Her frenemies situation with Sean aside, she liked these guys. And it was the one time in her week when she got to be around people who understood a whole side of her life that her civilian friends really couldn't.

Even in its quietest moments, going to war was a visceral experience that couldn't be fully understood without going through it. It was living under the constant threat of violence. It was constantly knowing your actions could lead to life or death for others—men and women you cared about and who were counting on you to have their backs. It was a head game that forever changed how your brain assessed and handled stress, threats, and even basic day-to-day sensory input—noises, smells, flashes of light.

"Yeah, I'll be there."

Mo nodded. "Good. Now go kick some more ass." He winked at her.

Dani managed a chuckle, then got in one of the lines for the spinning side kick drills they were running.

And she began planning the apology she owed to Sean that she knew he would hold over her until the end of time. That didn't mean she didn't owe it, though.

CHAPTER TWO

HURTING other people seemed to be Sean Riddick's fuckin' specialty.

Standing in the shower, he braced his hands against the wall, closed his eyes, and let the scalding water rain down on him. The other guys were laughing and talking as everyone cleaned up after WFC, but he could barely hear it for how his brain kept replaying the gasp of pain Dani made when he punched her. The way the light golden brown of her face went pale. How her arm instinctively cradled her side.

Daniela England was tough as nails. No question. But Sean was a fuckin' tank. And he should've known better than to allow his aggression to ramp up in response to hers.

And that was to say nothing of the way he'd taken her to the mats. He wasn't sure why he'd done that—

Scratch that. He knew exactly why he'd done that. They'd been in that clinch. And her cheeks had gone flush and her lips had parted, her gaze latching onto his mouth.

Whatever that moment of desire was had unleashed something inside him. Something he'd kept boxed up where Dani was concerned ever since their one night together eight months before.

Sheer base animal need.

That was why he'd done it. It didn't matter to his body that Daniela didn't like him nor that he tired of her ball-busting him all the damn time. And his cock didn't give a shit if Sean himself hadn't ever had a real relationship because he was convinced that he was destined to hurt those around him.

Nope. None of that seemed to matter when Sean got close to Dani. Because that night he'd spent with her was quite possibly the best he'd ever felt in his whole miserable life.

"Yo, Riddick, you need us to send the Coasties in after you or what?" Billy called out to a round of laughter.

"Fuck all y'all," he responded, turning off the water. He ran his hands over his face, then grasped the towel and gave himself a quick onceover before securing the terrycloth around his waist.

"There he is," Mo said when Sean turned the corner to the group of lockers where the other guys, mostly dressed already, were hanging out. Among them were Mo, Billy Parrish, and Noah Cortez, the three guys Sean knew best of anyone in the club. Jesse Anderson was also there, a WFC newbie and fellow prior navy guy like himself who Sean liked a lot.

"You look beat," Billy said. Parrish had been an Army Ranger who now worked as a private investigator, and while they'd known each other for about two years through WFC, it was only in the past few months that they'd finally gotten closer. Largely because Billy's girlfriend, Shayna, brought them together. Last fall, she'd witnessed and been the first photojournalist on the scene of a four-alarm apartment-building fire caused by a natural gas explosion. And Sean's company had been called to the scene, which was how he learned that Shayna was hurt but still doing her job and helping the residents out, too. After it was all over, working that fire had brought the three of them closer. Crisis did that, sometimes. "You okay?"

Tugging on his jeans, Sean nodded. "Yeah. Just didn't get much sleep last night."

"Work?" Mo asked.

Sean pulled on a shirt then sat his ass on the bench to put on his shoes and socks. "Yeah. We got a bullshit false alarm at two thirty. Couldn't fall back to sleep after that." Only good news was that he wasn't scheduled again until Tuesday, so he had a few days to recuperate. That was the beauty of a firefighter's schedule—ten twenty-four-hour days a month and he was done. Although, in practice, Sean picked up as many additional shifts as he could. And why not? He didn't have a wife or kids or other family obligations like a lot of the guys.

Nope, he didn't have anyone at all.

"Well, some food will help," Noah said. The former Marine had joined WFC at the same time Tara had last year, but he fit in so well it was like he'd always been here. "Where are we going anyway? I think Kristina might join and I gotta text her."

"Oh, yeah?" Billy said. "Shayna's coming, too."

"That's perfect," Noah said. "I know Kristina and Shayna wanted to talk about the menu for our big July 4th shindig."

Sean shook his head. "I think I'm sitting this one out."

"Wait. What?" As if he wasn't sure he'd heard Sean right, Noah turned his head to bring his good right ear closer to the conversation. He'd experienced a partial loss of vision and hearing on his left side—another war-borne demon. God knew they all had them. "You're not coming to July 4th?"

"No, no, I wouldn't miss that. I mean dinner. I'm out," Sean said.

"No way, Riddick." Billy frowned at him. "I already told Shayna you'd be there."

He shrugged. "I'm shit for company right now."

"We're all shit for company sometimes, son," Mo said, rising from the far end of the bench. "You'll fit right in just like always."

Dani's flinch played before his mind's eye again, and Sean had no idea if he could even stomach food right now. Because hurting her was only the most recent time in his life that he'd fucked up and gotten someone hurt.

Mo stepped right in front of him. "Besides, if you don't come, I'm gonna be fucking outnumbered. It'll just be me and all these lovebirds over here with their better halves"—he thumbed toward Noah, Billy, and Jesse.

"Dani and Jayne are coming, too, Mo," Billy said, smirking. "So you can hang with the ladies if our PDAs get to be too much." Everyone chuckled.

I'm no fucking lady.

The memory almost made Sean smile. Because Daniela England was many things, but a proper lady she was not. And that was no knock on her. Because Dani was part angel and part fuckin' warrior. A nurse who'd flown into combat zones on helicopters routinely targeted by enemy antiaircraft fire. And now an ER nurse in one of DC's busiest hospitals. Still getting up and going every day, and doing real good in the world, all despite losing her husband.

Daniela England might've been a stubborn, sharp-tongued ball-buster who somehow knew how to push every one of his buttons, but he couldn't deny that she was also a badass. Who he'd still managed to hurt.

And since she'd been pissed at the end of their drill, no doubt she'd prefer he wasn't at dinner. Which, fine. All things considered, he wasn't up for more of her digs at him tonight anyway. She always seemed to know how to crawl under his skin, and he was already raw enough as it was.

Sean rose and clapped Mo on the arm. "The ladies are all

yours, big guy." He grabbed his helmet from his locker and shut the door with a resounding metallic *clank.*

"Shit, Riddick, you're really not coming?" Billy asked.

"Nah. Another time, man." They all left the locker room, and found Dani, Tara, and Jayne waiting by the doors.

"About time, ladies," Dani called. The fuckin' ball-buster. It almost made him smile.

"How the heck did we get ready faster than you?" Tara asked with wide eyes. "Again."

Some good-natured ribbing got flung back and forth, but Dani was all Sean knew in that moment. At first, he had to look at her to make sure she was okay. And, truth be told, she seemed completely fine. But close on the heels of that observation was taking note for the millionth time of how fuckin' gorgeous she was, dressed casually now in a pair of skinny dark-wash jeans and a royal blue shirt that set off her flashing black eyes and silky black hair, down from the braid she'd worn earlier.

Before Daniela, he'd never known a woman that both drove him up a wall and to his fuckin' knees. Now, he routinely struggled between wanting to take that smart mouth down a notch or two or kiss the sarcasm out of her. For starters.

None of which was helped by remembering just how damn good they'd been together, even though that one time had been in his truck. He'd playfully grabbed her when she'd punched him and their bodies had collided, and then it'd been like they'd both let themselves off of some kind of leash. Need had roared through him, and he'd kissed her. And he'd never been kissed back more enthusiastically in his entire goddamn life. Getting inside his truck was all they'd been able to do before hands and mouths had wandered *all kinds* of interesting places. Places, sometimes in his dreams, he could still taste.

But all of that was their little secret. None of their friends had the slightest idea they'd hooked up, which was just how it should be. Especially since nothing would ever come of it anyway.

Blinking out of the thought, Sean followed as they moved up to the main floor as a group, then exited through the lobby with its case of trophies and medals and the industrial-looking registration desk. The warmth of the summer night air, heavy with mugginess from the frequent rain lately, surrounded them as they spilled out in front of Full Contact in the heart of DC's U Street neighborhood.

"So, the Moroccan place over in Adams Morgan? Is that what we decided?" Noah asked, his cell to his ear. Words of agreement rose up from the group as everyone headed in the direction of their cars.

"I'll see you all later," Sean called out, giving a wave.

"Wait, you're not coming?" Dani stepped back up on the sidewalk.

Helmet under his arm, he was already retreating to where his bike was parked around the corner. "Why? You gonna miss me?" Given how he felt, he didn't deliver the line with his usual bravado and it fell flat.

"You wish," she said, but the comeback also fell flat. As if she were reading lines rather than really trying to get in a dig.

He shook his head. "Nope. You get a Sean-free night, so never say I didn't do something nice for ya, Dani." He threw her a wink. Humor was always a good way to cover up all kinds of bullshit, wasn't it?

"Oh. Okay," she said.

He wasn't sure what to make of her hesitation, or of the way she turned away and then back again, like she had something else to say, but he wasn't particularly itching for another fight at the moment, so he ducked his head and kept going.

With all the rain lately, he hadn't been able to ride his bike as much as he preferred—instead, he'd been driving his truck most of the time, which was still full of memories of Dani. Her body. Her skin. Her moans. So when he'd left for WFC and the weather had been clear, he'd jumped on the chance to get a few hours on the back of his Harley. Riding and working on upgrades of his Sportster Iron 883 were two of his favorite hobbies—and two more things that helped get him out of his head.

Always a good thing.

He mounted up, tugged on a pair of gloves, and secured his helmet, then turned the key and smiled as the engine came to life beneath him. He fuckin' loved this bike, not to mention the feeling of freedom he got with nothing between him and the wind.

Sean eased the bike out of his space and onto the one-way side street, twisting the throttle as he approached the green light and prepared to swing a left-hand turn.

It all slowed down from there, once he was mid-intersection and it was too late to change the trajectory of his bike or his decision. He caught the too-fast movement at his left from the corner of his eye. Looked to see the truck not stopping for the red light. Knew there was no fuckin' way he wasn't going to get hit.

The pattern on the rectangular grill came right for him.

Sean corrected as best he could to turn himself out of the way.

But he didn't think it was going to be enough.

And then it wasn't.

———

"SEAN!" Dani yelled from where she'd been standing on the corner, debating talking to him now since he wasn't going to dinner. But then the truck and the screeching brakes and the crunching collision of metal against metal against wet, hard pavement...

Heart in her throat, she took off at a sprint. Off the curb. Around where the truck had belatedly skidded to a stop. "Oh, God." Sean's bike lay in a heap, it's whole back end badly mangled. And Sean lay a good ten feet away from it, face down.

Not moving.

"Jesus, Sean, are you okay?" She dropped to her knees beside him. When he didn't respond, she tried again. "Can you hear me, Sean?"

Nothing.

Stomach rolling, she grasped his wrist. His pulse was fast and strong, and the relief of feeling that forceful beat might've taken her to her knees if she weren't already there. She fished her cell phone out of her purse and dialed 9-1-1.

Heavy footsteps ran up behind her, then Mo was right there. "Fuck, how is he?"

She held up a hand as the dispatcher picked up. "My name's Daniela England and I'm an ER nurse at University Hospital. I need an ambulance at 13th and W streets, Northwest. A box truck ran a red light and struck a man on a motorcycle. Thirty-two and otherwise healthy. He's unconscious but has a strong pulse."

"Okay, Daniela. We have another report about this incident and already have an ambulance en route," the dispatcher said. "Are there any visible injuries?"

Dani's gaze ran over Sean's strong body—his *too-still* body. One of his hands was banged up through the shredded remains of a glove, but that was all she could see. "A few abrasions are visible, but nothing else. He was wearing a helmet, but he's lying on his stomach and I don't want to turn him without a spinal evaluation." Just saying those words made Dani want to puke. What if—

No. *No*. This wasn't her friend, Sean. Or whatever they were. This was a patient. *Get your head in the game, Dani*.

When she heard the sirens in the distance, she hung up with the dispatcher, which was the first time she noticed the crowds of people that had gathered on the sidewalk.

"They're almost here," Mo said. "Fucking hell."

"It was like watching a disaster unfold knowing what the outcome would be but unable to prevent it," Dani said.

Mo's face was pinched with worry. "I only heard it, but it didn't sound good. I was only still here because I got a call. I think everyone else left for the restaurant."

Dani nodded. "Mind going to see if the truck driver is injured?"

Mo squeezed her shoulder as he got to his feet.

She bent closer to Sean's head. "Sean? Can you hear me? I need you to wake up." She placed her hand lightly on his shoulder. "Come on, Riddick, you stubborn asshole, wake the fuck up and do something annoying."

A low groan from deep in his throat.

The surprised sound she made was part laugh and part cry. "That's it. Wake up now," she said.

Mo returned to her side. "Driver said he's not hurt."

Dani nodded up at him. "Sean's coming to."

Mo's eyes went wide and he dropped to his knees. "Come on, son. We need you awake," he said, voice gritty with concern.

On a grunt, Sean stretched out one of his legs and dragged a hand up as if he intended to push off the ground.

"Good, that's good, Sean. But don't try to move too much," she said, relief a tidal wave rolling through her. He wasn't paralyzed.

His fingers fumbled at his helmet. "Off," he croaked.

Just then, EMS arrived, a team she knew from seeing them at the ER—Mike Garcia and Erin Bronson. Dani let them know what she could—and who they were working on since there was a decent chance they'd know him, then backed out of the way enough to let them do their jobs.

"Whoa, whoa, Riddick," Garcia said as Sean tugged at his helmet. "Easy. Let us evaluate you first."

"They need to check out your neck and spine, Sean," Dani said, still kneeling in his line of sight.

"They're fuckin' fine," he said, almost making Dani laugh. Such a stubborn asshole.

She knelt closer. "Well, they're gonna fucking check. So fucking cooperate. Okay?"

He made a noise like a laugh, but it quickly turned into a cough. In a burst of effort, he shoved the helmet off. "Can't...breathe."

"Damnit, Riddick." But that was all Dani could say when she saw the giant crack that jagged all across the helmet's visor. A piece of the clear plastic had caved inward, and Sean had a corresponding bloody slice all along the side of his nose and running under his eyebrow. *Jesus.*

"We're going to turn you over using a spinal board," Garcia said.

Sean made a sound deep in his throat. "Fuck that—"

Bronson placed the board at Sean's back, her blond ponytail falling over her shoulder as she worked, and he elbowed it away and turned himself over, eliciting concern and protests from their whole group.

"Don't need it. I'm tellin' ya my spine's fine," Sean said. "All ten fingers and toes are doing their thing. It's just, you know, everything else that fuckin' hurts."

Mo bent over so that he was staring down directly above their friend's bloodied face. "You listen to me, son, and you listen good. You're going to cooperate with these fine people or the second you're upright again I'm going to beat the shit out of you."

Sean groaned. "*Fine.*"

The word pulled Dani back into their earlier exchange, which she felt even worse about now. Shit. "Why do first responders make such terrible patients?" she snarked, smirking at Sean to try to distract him from everything else.

Garcia slanted her a glance and winked. The blue-eyes-and-dark-hair combo was just one of the reasons he was popular at the ER. Luckily, he was also damn good at his job, which Dani was seeing firsthand. "Doctors and nurses aren't much better," he said.

Sean laughed and nearly coughed up a lung again. "Always did like you, Garcia."

"Shut up, asshole." Garcia grinned as he threaded an oxygen line under Sean's nose and around his ears.

The good-natured banter rushed more relief through Dani. Sean was moving. He was talking. He was being his usual sarcastic self. She'd never been happier about that.

"My vision's all fucked up," Sean said waving at his bloody eye.

While Bronson patched up Sean's hands, Garcia flashed a light in Sean's eyes and frowned. "Unilateral dilated pupil, left side."

Dani bit back a curse. Given his injury, she wasn't surprised, but that wasn't great.

"Fuck, that doesn't sound good," Sean said, echoing her thoughts. "What does that mean?"

"What can you see?" Garcia asked.

"It's all blurry on that side. What's it mean?"

Garcia secured gauze over the eye. "It's common when there's trauma to the eye. They'll be able to give you more info at the hospital."

"Fuck, Mike, I gotta be able to see the fires to fight 'em."

A rock sank into Dani's gut as Mike replied the only way he could: "We're gonna take care of you, buddy."

The EMTs stepped away to get the stretcher, and Dani leaned in. "All I want you thinking about is staying calm and getting better. We'll figure the rest out."

"I gotta be able to see, D."

She swallowed around a knot of emotion. "It's not time to worry, Sean. Not yet. I promise."

"You'll tell me. Right? You'll tell me when it is?" He nailed her with a one-eyed stare that was just south of panicked.

"I'll fucking tell you," she said, playing it hard and cool so he would believe she wasn't scared. That everything was cool, normal, totally *fine*.

That word again.

Garcia and Bronson returned, and Dani almost groaned when she saw what Mike had in his hands.

"We don't need to transport you on the spinal board, but you do need the collar—"

Sean's jaw went tight. "No, I don't—"

Mo leaned over him again. "Wear the damn collar." Sean gave in and Garcia got busy putting it on.

Bronson smirked up at Mo. "You wanna come on all our calls?" The big guy chuffed out something that, under other circumstances, might've turned into a full-on laugh. Then his cell rang and he stepped away.

Dani rose and suddenly there were cops there wanting to talk to her. Keeping one eye on Sean as they prepared to load him up, she gave her information and a quick run-down of what she saw.

"Look, I'm riding with him to the hospital. Is there any chance you can follow up there? Or can I call you tomorrow?" Dani asked the policewoman.

"The driver admitted that he didn't see the light, so we might not need more from you, but I have your information just in case." The woman handed Dani a business card.

"Thank you," she said, slipping it into her jeans pocket. Dani turned to Mike and Erin. "I'm riding along." When the EMTs nodded, she looked for Mo and founded him standing at the edge of the crowd, where all their friends stood huddled. When had they gotten here? She jogged over.

"How is he?" Billy asked just as Shayna said, "Is he okay?"

"Better than I expected. Banged up and having some vision issues in one eye from a cut. The visor to his helmet caved in."

"Jesus," Noah said, with Kristina tucked tight beside him. "That helmet probably saved his life."

Dani nodded, itching to get back to Sean's side. "Listen, they're taking him to University. I'm riding in the ambulance."

"Go. We'll see you over there," Mo said.

With that Dani rushed to the open rear door and climbed up into the rig. Garcia was at the wheel, and Bronson was busy getting the stretcher secured and Sean hooked up to everything he needed to be hooked up to.

"I need you belted in, too," Erin said to her.

Dani was already doing it. It wasn't a helicopter, of course, but the same safety protocols applied and her muscle memory kicked in to secure herself. And then she reached out to Sean. She wasn't sure how to touch him in a way that wouldn't hurt, so she rested her hand on his wrist.

His gaze cut to her. "Do I know how to show a woman a good time on a Saturday night or what?" The words were full of humor even as the storm roiling in his dark-eyed gaze wasn't.

"If you wanted to get me alone, you could've just asked," she said with a smirk.

"You would've cut me off at the knees."

"Damn straight." She squeezed his arm and her thumb

rubbed back and forth just to take a little of the bite out of the words.

"Don't get soft on me now, Dani," he said, his voice like sandpaper had scoured his throat. She didn't need him to explain that. The minute she got soft with him, he'd know something was really wrong.

It took fifteen minutes to get across town to the hospital, and they rode the rest of the way in silence.

Whatever the weird nature of their drive-each-other-fucking-crazy status was, Dani was glad that she could be there for Sean.

Even if being there for a man she sometimes wanted to strangle made her feel even worse for not having been there for the man she'd loved.

CHAPTER THREE

It wasn't often that Dani found herself in the hospital's waiting room as a visitor, and she freaking hated it. She'd stayed with Sean long enough to get him admitted and triaged, long enough to see them cut off his shirt so they could examine his abdomen, long enough for the team to determine he needed a CT scan to both check for a head injury and evaluate the orbital trauma.

Which was where he was now.

At least she had everyone from WFC here waiting with her. Mo sat with a cup of coffee in his hands that she hadn't seen him once drink. Kristina sat with her head against Noah's shoulder, both of her hands wrapped tight around one of his as if she were holding him together. And Dani guessed by the way Noah's knee was bouncing that maybe Kris was doing just that. Over meals and other get-togethers this past year, Dani had gotten to know Kristina Moore, and it was clear how much strength Noah drew from her. Given how wrecked Noah had been when he'd first joined WFC, Dani knew their relationship had started off rocky. But to look at them now, you'd never know it.

Her gaze moved next to Billy and Shayna. His elbows resting on his knees, his hands slack, his head hanging down. The position exposed some of the burn scars on the back of his neck from an explosion that had taken out a lot of his Ranger unit. Dani had been out of the army by the time that'd happened, but she still knew enough people in the service that word sometimes got to her. And since she'd worked on more than a few Rangers over the years, word of the ambush that had killed Billy's teammates made its way to her before she'd ever even met him. Next to him, Shayna sat with her hand massaging the back of Billy's neck, her fingers occasionally stroking the ends of his hair.

Shayna tucked her dark hair behind an ear and unleashed a long sigh. "Come on, Sean." The whispered plea made the backs of Dani's eyes prick. Last fall, Shayna and Sean had worked a disaster together—her as a journalist and him as a fire-fighter—and something about that experience had forged almost a sibling type of closeness between them.

Opposite them, Tara sat on a couch, her back resting against Jesse's chest. Their hands were entangled and resting against Tara's belly. Tara's head leaned against her free hand and her eyes were closed, but the tension in her posture made it clear she wasn't resting. Every so often, Jesse pressed a kiss to her hair.

The couples weren't doing anything out of the ordinary for lovers, but fuck if they weren't making something inside Dani ache, something that she didn't even want to think about let alone feel. Six years ago, she'd packed away the part of her that needed the kind of quiet yet fundamental intimacy that came from sharing life and love with another person. And she wanted that need to *stay* all put away.

Next to Shayna, Coach Mack and Jayne sat in that silently

restless way that came from waiting to know if someone you cared about was going to be okay.

Dani got up and paced. *Come on*, she shouted inside her head. *Come fucking tell us his vision is going to be okay already.* She tugged her hair into a ponytail and tilted her head back, and then let the long strands go again, just to have something to do with her hands.

"Dani?" Jayne said, rising from her seat. "Will you give me a call and let me know what's going on? I should probably get home to check on Dad."

"Yeah, of course," she said, rubbing Jayne's arm. "We'll make sure Sean knows you were here."

She nodded. "I'm praying for him."

"Thanks." Dani hugged herself as Jayne said good-bye to the others. Despite the June heat, a chill had seeped into her bones while she'd been on the street with Sean. The cold air conditioning of the waiting room wasn't helping, and she'd left her sweater in her car still parked back at Full Contact.

After Jayne left, Mo got to his feet.

"You heading out?" Dani asked.

"Hell, no," he said. "My ass is just getting tired of sitting." That pronouncement gave rise to a round of chuckles.

"Do they make the chairs uncomfortable on purpose?" Billy asked, shifting back in his seat. He pulled Shayna's hand to his mouth and kissed her knuckles.

Dani looked away.

"Why don't I go down to the cafeteria and get some drinks and snacks," Tara said.

"That's a good idea," Kristina said. "I'll come with you to help carry things if you want."

Tara nodded. "Sure. Any special requests?"

When the guys didn't answer, Shayna said, "We could probably all use some sugar and caffeine. So whatever fits that bill."

"Want help?" Jesse asked, concern filling those dark eyes. Because of their navy backgrounds, he and Sean had gotten tight these past few months. Dani was glad that Sean had so many people here rooting for him.

"We got it," Tara said with a small smile. "But you're welcome to tag along."

Jesse got to his feet. "Maybe if we leave, news will come faster." Murmurs of agreement went around the circle, and then the three of them left.

On a sigh, Mo stopped pacing and nailed her with a dark-eyed stare. "Lay it out for us, Dani. What's going on right now?"

She took a deep breath and met each expectant gaze in the room as she spoke. "They're gonna be most concerned with evaluating the injury to his eye. They'll check for fractures to the bony orbit, note any herniations to the parts of the eye, check the position of the lens, and look for bleeds and foreign bodies. They'll also make sure the optic nerves weren't impacted. And I would have to think he has a concussion, so they'll give his whole hard head a once-over, too."

"Finally, one time him being hardheaded comes in handy," Billy said, raking a hand through his dark blond hair.

"Amen to that." Mo managed a chuckle.

Noah wiped his hands hard against his thighs. "I hate hospitals."

"Fuckin' A," Billy said. "No offense, Dani."

She chuffed out a laugh because she couldn't blame them, especially as both Noah and Billy had spent considerable time in hospitals as patients. Billy for his burns, and Noah for the head injury that had reduced his hearing and sight on one side. Which, now that she thought of it, was probably why Tara seemed kinda tense, too. No one ended up in WFC that hadn't been chewed up and spit back out by war. "None taken, believe me."

Just then, Tara, Jesse, and Kristina returned with two plastic bags of goodies—cans of soda, bags of chips and pretzels, and candy and granola bars. "Dinner is served," Tara said.

Dani grabbed a can of ginger ale hoping it might help settle her unsettled gut.

"You should eat something, too," Tara said gently. "It's probably going to be a long night, right? It'll be easier with some fuel on board. That goes for everyone."

"Yes, Mom," Mo said.

Tara smacked his arm. "Put something in that pie hole, Moses Griffin." That got him to chuckle, and Dani thought that anything that could inject some humor was all to the good.

Appreciating what Tara was trying to do, Dani grabbed a bag of pretzels.

Another half hour passed before one of her colleagues poked her head into the waiting room. "Dani?"

She was on her feet and across the room in an instant. "How is he?"

Dr. Sarah Mitchell was one of Dani's favorite docs. Short with white-blond hair and nearly violet eyes, she was young, aggressively advocated for her patients, and always listened to the nurses. "He's doing good. Resting. Does he have any family here?"

"No. None local," Dani said.

From right behind her, Billy cleared his throat. "His Dad lives in Philly and isn't well. I wasn't sure whether to try to get in touch with him until we knew more, especially since they're not close." Dani blinked. She didn't know any of that.

Dr. Mitchell nodded and looked to Dani. "He asked for you to be present when I went over everything."

Heart tripping into a sprint, Dani turned to the others. "I'll fill you in as soon as I can."

Mo nodded. "Tell him we're all here for him."

"I will," Dani said, following the doc through the big double doors. It was a short walk to his exam room, where she found Sean propped up in bed wearing a blue hospital gown and an IV. An oblong eye shield covered his injured eye. "Hey, Sean."

"Hey, girl, hey," he said in a sing-song that was totally not him. Jesus, he was high as a kite.

"Enjoying some pain meds, I see," she said, biting back her humor. It certainly made sense why he wanted her in here now.

"Don't I make this gown look good?"

Dani laughed under her breath. "Sure, dude. Whatever you say."

Dr. Mitchell pulled up a stool. "So here's the deal. About your eye injury. All the orbital structures appear intact. The cut along the orbital rim fortunately wasn't deep, but it did require fifteen stitches."

The news made Dani feel like she could breathe again. The guy might drive her fucking nuts, but she'd never wish him harm. And she knew how much being a firefighter meant to him —the same thing being a nurse meant to her: helping people, making the world just a little better one day at a time, tipping the *do-no-harm* balance sheet a little in the right direction.

The doctor continued. "The blurriness you're experiencing is likely from the blunt force trauma caused by how you landed. The hope is that time will reduce the inflammation causing the blurriness."

Sean's gaze swung to where Dani stood at the foot of his bed. "The *hope*...? D?"

"It's good news. No reason to worry yet."

"You'd tell me?"

"Absolutely."

Dr. Mitchell nodded. "Dani's right. You also have a concussion and some bruising to your lungs, which is why you were having some difficulty breathing. Chest wall injuries can make it painful to breathe, laugh, cough, or lift things. You might also have pain or stiffness in your shoulders or back. All of which should clear up on its own in the next couple weeks."

Dani nodded, mentally ticking off things he was going to need or need to do after discharge. There would be prescriptions to fill, follow-up visits to attend, schedules to rearrange, and help he might need until the chest pain dissipated enough for him to be lifting or bending.

"When can I go back to work?" Sean asked.

"You're a firefighter?" Dr. Mitchell asked. Dani mentally cringed—there was no way he was going to like her answer. When Sean nodded, the doc continued, "Assuming your vision and chest pain clears up, I would think you could get back to work in three or four weeks, depending on your pain level and recovery."

Sean blanched. "*Four weeks?*"

"All things considered, you were pretty lucky tonight, Mr. Riddick. But your injuries are going to take some time to heal." Dr. Mitchell rose. "We're going to keep you overnight to see how your eye progresses, so they'll be moving you upstairs soon."

"Thanks, Doc," Sean managed as she left. He dropped his head back against the bed.

Dani took up the doc's seat on the stool. "I know it's a lot, but it's good news, Sean."

He blew out a breath that sent him into a coughing fit. He curled into himself trying to avoid the pain of it.

"I'm going to get you another pillow. If you hug it when you need to cough, it makes it hurt less." She put a hand on his knee. "Be right back, okay?"

"Yeah," he managed.

She went to retrieve the pillow, and several of the other nurses stopped her along the way.

"Hope your friend's okay, Dani," one said.

"I'm praying for your friend," said another.

"I was sorry to hear about your friend, Dani," a third called. *Friend.* In that moment, she had no problem thinking of Sean Riddick that way.

"Thanks," Dani said each time. She returned to his room to find his eyes closed, so she eased the pillow down next to him and returned to the waiting room to fill the others in and tell them they might as well head home since Sean was being admitted.

Not that Dani was going anywhere. No, *this time* she wasn't missing a chance to be there.

Sometimes, atonement was all you had, even if you could never truly atone for the things you did wrong.

FUUUUUCK.

That was Sean's first thought upon waking to the gray light of morning spilling through the window of his hospital room. Every fucking thing hurt.

His face. His head. His chest. His back. His hands.

The mental calculus went on long enough that he decided he should catalog what *didn't* hurt... His feet, thanks to the pair of shitkickers he'd been wearing. And his dick, thanks to God.

Bleary eyed, he lifted his head, then blinked twice. Because the pain was making him hallucinate. Either that or he was actually seeing Daniela curled up asleep in a chair across the room. Her expression relaxed, her hair like a shawl of black silk all around her shoulders, her face so damn pretty.

Why was she here?

Swallowing made him feel like he'd spent the night walking through a desert, so he reached for the Styrofoam cup with a bendy straw sticking up through its lid that was sitting on the rolling table next to his bed. But the fucking bandages on his hand made it so that he couldn't grab the damn thing. Worse, he knocked it over trying.

"Damnit," he said, instinctively lurching to catch it.

Which, holy shit, was the wrooooong goddamned thing to do. He grunted against the pain, which threw him into a coughing fit that made his chest feel like he'd been recently body-slammed by a box truck. A scorching hot pain exploded through his lungs until he was clutching his pecs and balling up.

A hand on his shoulder. Soothing words in his ear he couldn't quite make out over the roar in his head. A pillow pushed into his arms that provided an easing counterpressure.

"Jesus," Sean finally rasped, struggling to breathe and trying to avoid breathing deeply all at the same time. "What the fuck."

"Chest wall injuries are a bitch," Dani said, standing right behind him.

He peered up at her with his one good eye. "No shit."

She smirked. "I won't bother asking how you're feeling."

Hugging the pillow, he slowly rolled back against the bed. The effort it took made him swallow hard, but his throat was so dry it hurt.

Dani didn't have to be asked. She brought the straw of the cup to his mouth. He moaned at the cool relief it brought. Even though, Jesus, he was fucking useless. And what that meant for his life—and his job—for the immediate future was a blow that had yet to fully kick his ass. But he knew it was going to. Sooner rather than later. Because idle time was not his friend.

He drank so long that he was nearly panting by the time he let go of the straw and came up for air. "Thanks," he managed.

She nodded, then made quick work of wiping up the water he'd spilled. "Most of WFC was here until about two A.M. I finally had to kick everyone out of the hospital or else they'd have racked out in the waiting room. They all wanted you to know they were here though."

He studied her as she busied herself with the spill and straightening up his tray and looking over his flashing vitals on the machines that sat off to the side. "So why are you here?"

Her gaze snapped to his, and he immediately regretted the question, especially as her usual guardedness replaced the softness he'd seen in her eyes just a moment before. She retreated a step from the edge of his bed and nailed him with a stare. "You asked me to stay."

Asshole.

She hadn't said that, but he heard it all the same. And he deserved it, too. Fuck, he hadn't meant the question to sound the way it did. As if he didn't want her there, when really he just couldn't figure out why she was. Or why she'd agreed even if he'd asked. After all, before that truck took him for a spin, Sean had fuckin' hurt her. "Ignore me. I'm an asshole."

She rolled her eyes. "You don't say. I think I liked you better when you were high."

He searched his brain for what she was talking about but came up empty. A lot after the too-close image of that truck's grill was a blank at the moment...

Dani crossed her arms, putting up another line of defense. "Let's just say you were channeling Ryan Gosling."

He frowned. "Gosling? You mean Reynolds? Was I was quoting 'Deadpool'?" Shit, he couldn't remember that at all.

That actually got a little laugh out of her. "You can quote 'Deadpool'?"

Hell, yeah, he could. "If I ever decide to become a crime-fighting shit swizzler who rooms with a bunch of other little whiners at Neverland Mansion with some creepy, old, bald, Heaven's Gate-looking motherfucker, on that day, I'll send your shiny, happy ass a friend request." He was breathing a little hard by the end of the line, but it still made him grin—well as close to a grin as he could manage given how he felt.

Dani blinked. Then made a face. "That's 'Deadpool'?"

Inside his head, Sean heard a record scratch. "Are you fuckin' telling me you haven't seen 'Deadpool'?" Just that little bit of excitement had him grasping his chest. "Fuck, this sucks."

"I know," she said. "And nope, I haven't."

"Your 'Deadpool' inexperience is literally killing me. And unlike Wade, I won't come back to life."

She frowned, confusion plain on her face. "You're saying words, but I have no idea what they mean."

"Jesus Christmas. 'Deadpool' is a goddamn masterpiece."

Dani shook her head. "I don't know what to tell ya."

"That is unsat, D. Unfuckingsat."

A nurse in pink scrubs breezed into the room. "Well, good morning, Mr. Riddick. You're looking better today." The older woman smiled at Daniela. "Hi, Dani, how are ya, hon?"

"Hi, Patricia," Dani said, moving toward the end of the bed as if to get out of the way.

"I feel like I got hit by a truck," Sean said, trying to smile at the lady.

"A box truck, the way I hear it," Patricia said, giving him a wink before she busied herself noting down his vitals. "Can you tell me where your pain is at on a scale of zero to ten, with ten being the worst in your life?"

He glanced at Dani, then down at his hands again. "Eh, maybe a four."

"And how about when you cough?" Dani asked. Her voice was completely neutral, so why did he feel like she was challenging him?

He frowned. "I don't know. Maybe a five."

Her eyes called *bullshit* so damn loud.

"Or a six. When will we know something about my eye?" He cared far more about that.

"The doc will be here in a while," the nurse said. "He'll be able to tell you more. In the meantime, I'll get you some more pain medication."

"That's okay. I can manage without it," he said. The nurse gave him a look. And damnit if Dani wasn't giving him the same look. But he didn't want to rely on pain meds. He knew too many guys who'd had trouble getting off them once they started.

It was Dani who spoke. "Sean, you need to stay ahead of the pain with meds for at least the first few days. You're not feeling the full impact of that chest wall injury yet because you have meds in your system."

He sighed. Debated. But didn't have the energy to fight. "Fine."

The nurse nodded. "I'll be right back."

"Thanks." He blew out a frustrated breath as Patricia left the room, then reached for his cup, belatedly remembering his useless hands. "Fuck, I should've asked if these bandages could come off. Or are my paws stitched up, too?"

Dani held his water cup again as she said, "No stitches, just lots of abrasions."

He released the straw and caught a drip of water on his chin with the gauze on the back of his hand. "Thanks. Can we look then? Not even being able to suck a straw on my own is a pain in the ass."

"It's not the sucking that's your problem. It's the holding the cup." She reached out a hand toward one of his.

A slow grin tugged at his face. "You're right. I'm good at the sucking." He waggled his one eyebrow. He might be fucked up at the moment, but he never could pass up an opportunity for some good innuendo. And maybe given his current condition, she'd give him a little leeway on it.

She blinked, then rolled her eyes, but the pink that bloomed on the warm tan skin of her face belied her effort at disdain. Dani liked to play that he didn't affect her, but he damn well knew that he did. Just like she affected him. "Fuck sake," Dani muttered under her breath.

That made him chuckle. And *that* made him cough. He hugged the pillow to his chest with one arm.

Dani cradled his other hand in her palm. "Serves you right. I literally don't care what you're good at."

She didn't say he *wasn't* good, though, and that released a probably ridiculous masculine satisfaction through his blood. Because she *knew* damn right well that he could suck like a goddamned champ—a champ that had given her two orgasms with his mouth while she was spread out over the bench seat of his truck. Amused despite hacking up a lung, he watched her unwind the length of gauze until he finally regained his breath. "I got skills, D. As you well know. That's all I'm sayin'."

Even the glare she threw him couldn't quite hide her humor. Or the knowingness in her eyes. "You've got a ridiculous ego. That's all I'm saying."

Enjoying the banter, he grinned and met her gaze head on. "Well earned, baby girl. Well. Fucking. Earned."

"Call me that again and I'll punch your other eye, baby boy." She arched a brow at him. "Hear how ridiculous that sounds?"

He chuffed out an almost-laugh as the last of the gauze on his left hand fell away, and Sean took a gander at the damage. Someone had taken a cheese grater to the knuckles on the back of his hand, and the cuts stung when he tried to make a fist. Otherwise, his lefty was in decent shape. "And this was with gloves on."

"The hit really sent you flying," she said, unwrapping his other hand.

Surprised, his gaze cut to her. "You saw it?"

Without meeting his gaze, she nodded. "Yeah. I was coming to talk to you, but you'd already pulled into the street. So I was at the corner when it happened. I knew he was going to hit you but couldn't do a goddamn thing."

Competing thoughts erupted in Sean's head. What had she wanted to talk to him about? Was she finally going to give him the dressing down he deserved for how hard he'd hit her? And, wait, she didn't think she'd helped him? She'd apparently stayed at his request and spent the whole fucking night sitting at his side.

He inhaled to speak just as she removed the second bandage —and a new doctor knocked on the door jamb.

"Ah, Mr. Riddick, you're awake," the man said, entering the room. "I'm Dr. Nassir." He did a double take at Dani. "Daniela, you're not on duty, are you?"

"No, Sean and I are friends. Either that, or I can't get enough of being here."

The guy chuckled as he washed his hands. Sean examined the chewed-up mess that were the knuckles on his right hand. He guessed he was lucky he hadn't broken a couple fingers.

"Hey, Doc. Hope this is okay," he said, holding up his unbandaged hands. "The gauze was making me crazy because I couldn't hold anything."

The man took a look. "The gauze will help keep the cuts clean. Given how deep some of them are, you might want to give it another day or two. But we can wrap them differently so they're not so bulky." The doc stepped closer. "Let's take a look at the eye while we're at it, shall we?"

Sean's heart tripped over itself. "Yeah."

"Do you want me to step out, Sean?" Dani asked.

No. The quickness and certainty of his reaction was a total gut check. Thing was, they might not get along half the time, but

Sean knew for certain that he could count on Dani to tell him the truth, so he didn't want her going anywhere. He peered around the doctor. "Not at all."

Nodding, she came around the other side of the bed, gaze intent on his now even uglier mug.

Removing the last of the tape, Dr. Nassir pulled the eye shield and gauze away.

Sean blinked against the light and had two competing reactions. First, his vision was fucking blurry. But, second, he had a sudden flash of clarity that told him it wasn't anywhere near as blurry as the night before. And, remembering that, he suddenly recalled an image of Dani kneeling on the street and talking to him. Encouraging him. And she thought she hadn't done anything for him?

"How is your vision?" the man said, disposing of the bandage.

Swallowing hard, Sean tried to focus on the man's name badge. Blurry. "Uh, better than last night, I think, but not all the way clear."

The doc nodded in that non-committal way doctors had. "Let me take a look," he said, reaching for a scope with a light on it.

Sean was about going crazy by the time the guy was done looking, because he wasn't saying a thing. "So, what do you think?"

"Definite improvement. Swelling is going down. I'm cautiously hopeful that your sight will return to normal or close to normal. In the meantime, you need to keep the eye covered to reduce strain and let it rest. I'll have the nurse come in and take care of your dressings. And I don't see any reason why we can't discharge you today."

"Can Dani do it?" Sean asked. "The bandages, I mean." His not-quite-right gaze cut to her. "If you don't mind." He didn't want to be surrounded by false cheer and hopeful platitudes. He wanted Dani's straight-shooting candor, brutal though it could be.

"Sure. Yes," she said.

"Very good." The doc nodded. "It'll probably be a few hours before discharge, but we'll get things underway."

"Thanks," Sean managed. When the man left, Sean looked to Dani, the question on the tip of his tongue.

She didn't make him ask. "It's very good news, Sean."

"'*Close* to normal', though—"

"Is what he has to say. No doctor is going to promise you'll be healed until you are."

He blew out a breath. "Yeah. Okay."

Just then, Patricia returned with a syringe that she inserted into his IV. It took less than a minute for the warm fuzzies to spread over him.

When they were alone again, Dani leaned in close. "Lay your head back and rest while I go get some supplies."

Sean didn't even try to resist. Two drinks of water, some banter, and an examination by the doctor had left his run-over ass exhausted. And the meds were lulling him to sleep.

"I'll be back." She made for the door.

"I'll be here," he managed, closing his eyes so he didn't have to face the reality that his sight was fucked up. And might stay that way.

CHAPTER FOUR

Dani returned to find that Sean's breakfast had been delivered. Not that he knew since the guy was sound asleep. She settled the bandages on the tray for later and dropped into the chair in the corner. And then she found herself staring at the man who so often drove her freaking nuts.

It was different seeing him this way. Obviously hurting but putting up a brave front. Understandably scared but trying to make her laugh. In no condition for...*anything*, but still flirting with her. Her gaze tracked over the curve of stitches that ran under his eyebrow and down the bridge of his nose. It wasn't just lucky that his vision would likely return. As close as that cut ran, it was lucky that he hadn't lost the eye. Period.

She retrieved her cell phone and debated whether it was too early to send texts, but came down on the side of thinking everyone would want to be updated. She created a group chat and tapped out a message.

Hey all. The latest on Sean. Improvement in his eye though still some blurriness. Being discharged in a few hours. Between the vision issues and the chest wall injury, he's probably going to need some help for the next week. I don't work until tomorrow morning and I have off on Thursday so I can handle that plus today and tonight. Let me know if you can help.

Dani hit *Send*, then dropped her head back against the chair. And wished she'd been able to be there for Anthony this way.

It was a ridiculous, self-defeating thought, really. She knew it was. Because Anthony had never made it into the emergency room. He'd never laid in a hospital bed so that someone could sit at his side while he slept. Even if she hadn't been out on a flight run, she never would've had the opportunity to do this for him. But no one ever accused guilt of being rational.

Tangled in thought, Dani twisted the silver feather ring she wore on her right middle finger. Granny had given it to her for her fifteenth birthday and Dani had rarely taken it off since. On the inside was inscribed the Kiowa word, "MAHYEHN," which meant "woman." Dani could still remember how grown up and special she'd felt when she opened the little box.

She peered out the window, out to where the June sun shined streams of white gold through the dancing jade leaves of a tree. The day had been equally brilliant when she'd lost Anthony, though there wasn't much green to speak of at Bagram. All these years later, Dani still couldn't decide if Mother Nature was being cruel or reassuring when the weather was so pretty in the midst of the emotional storm that tore apart her life.

God, that storm had raged inside her for so long. Long enough that her commanding officer had been forced to tell her she needed a leave of absence. Long enough that she'd finally realized that leave could never be long enough to allow her to do the job as well as she needed. So she'd gotten out of the army.

Afterward, she'd returned to Oklahoma to live with Nana in her childhood home because she hadn't known where else to go. But she'd felt detached from everything—from the brother- and sisterhood of the army, from the Kiowa community her granny had been her main connection to before she'd passed. Dani had not only lost a husband; she realized she'd lost so much of herself. Sometimes, that feeling resurfaced even now from how she'd closed herself off to so many things ever since.

Did you know how much you took with you when you left?

She'd first read that question in a book about grief, and it had sucker-punched her with the devastating clarity it shined on some of what she'd felt and thus had always stuck with her.

As had the motto of the grief group she'd gone to for a while: Keep fucking going. She'd been all about that for years now, which was why she had exactly one tattoo: the letters K.F.G. on the inside of her ring finger on her left hand. She'd gotten it the day she finally managed to take off her wedding ring, about eighteen months after Anthony died. Dani had seen it as switching out one promise for another. The promise to survive in exchange for the lives they'd pledged to each other.

The cell vibrated in her palm, jarring her out of her thoughts. A text from Billy.

I probably have more flexibility than the rest of you so I'll cover whatever anyone else can't.

Another text followed a minute later, from Mo this time. *I can handle evenings or nights any day.*

Dani managed a smile as she read the exchange. This was one of the things that military people did so well—come together no questions asked to take care of one of their own. None of them were active duty anymore, of course, but WFC had brought them together in the same way.

As a family. A found family.

Really, the only one Dani had since she'd lost both her parents young, her granny when she'd been in high school, her grandfather just before she'd graduated from the University of Oklahoma, and her nana, the grandmother who raised, her just eight months after Anthony—which was when she'd left Okla-homa and moved to D.C. She would never forget where she came from, but there was nothing left for her there anymore. Nothing but ghosts.

She'd made friends here among the hospital staff, of course, but she was still closer to some of her WFC friends than she was with anyone else.

"No!"

Sean's shout came out of nowhere. It catapulted Dani's heart into her throat and nearly made her drop her phone. The coughing fit that followed had him hugging a pillow to his chest as she flew to his side.

"Hey, you're okay," she said, imagining the memory of that truck coming at him was going to trouble his dreams for a while. Poor guy.

He finally sagged back against the inclined mattress, and for a second he looked a hundred years old. It was the cast of his eyes that gave that impression, and it tugged hard at something inside Dani's chest. "If you say so, D."

When had he ever given in on anything so easily? "I do. Or I'll kill your stubborn ass."

He chuffed out a humorless laugh. "Some of the best love stories start with a murder."

The phrase "love story" poked at the part of her brain responsible for her fight or flight reflex. "Uh, dude, your head took quite a hit if you think we're in a love story."

Sean winked, and while the little gesture read as amused, the rest of his face didn't quite follow. "Relax. It's from 'Deadpool'."

"How often do you quote that movie and I not realize that's what you're doing?" She asked the question because she was curious, but also because she wanted to steer them far, far away from the love story topic.

"Prolly a lot." He heaved as deep of a breath as he could, wincing as his lungs expanded. "Would you please get me some water?"

Did Sean Riddick just say *please*? Under any other circumstances, she would've razzed him for it or suspected him of wanting something. But there was nothing except sincerity in his voice.

Dani grabbed the cup and brought the straw to his lips. No jokes about sucking this time. No flirting or humor or brave front. It was like that nightmare had exposed all the hurt beneath those masks, and *that* thought made Dani want to help him. Sean never seemed anything but *strong* to her. His body, his personality, his bravery. Seeing him vulnerable kinda stole her breath with the wrongness of it.

So when he was done with his drink, she eased down onto the edge of his mattress, her hip against his. Still, he didn't meet her gaze. So she cupped the side of his face in her hand.

That dark gaze cut to meet hers. A wariness settled in alongside the pain he couldn't quite erase from his features.

"We got this. You hear me? You, me, all our friends. We're all going to get you through it."

Sean covered her hand with his and pressed his face more tightly to her palm. "Thanks, Daniela. Needed to hear that."

"Any time. Now let me get that eye bandaged back up."

"Yes, ma'am."

She smiled and got to work on his eye. "I could get used to that."

He managed a more Sean-like smirk. "Prolly shouldn't."

"I know."

He was quiet while she patched him up, and then he grasped her hand as she went to pull away. "Thanks, D. I mean it."

"Don't mention it. You'd do the same for me." Crazy

enough, that wasn't just a line. She knew without question that Sean would give her his own blood if she needed it. He was one of the helpers, as Mr. Rogers called them. It was what her granny had told her when her father had died in that accident. *"Look for the helpers. You'll always find people who are helping."* She'd never seen his television show before that, but she'd become a big fan after, because there *was* comfort in focusing on those trying to make a bad situation better. It was part of what made her want to become a nurse.

For a long moment, Sean ducked his chin. "You really believe that?"

Dani blinked, unable to figure out what he was talking about. Because the obvious topic was just too...impossible. But what else could it be? "Are you asking me if I believe you'd take care of me if I needed it?" He shrugged one big shoulder. It was all she could do to keep the *what-the-fuck* out of her expression. How could he even wonder? "Dude, just because you drive me batshit sometimes doesn't mean I don't know you're a fundamentally good person."

His uninjured eye flashed up to hers again. And there was a question there. Like he was assessing her sincerity. "Okay," he said, dropping his head back against the pillow.

Dani wanted to probe this, wanted to push. Had she been so much of a bitch to him that he could question such a thing? Fuck.

That line of inquiry reminded her that she still owed him an apology. So, yeah, maybe she *had*. She inhaled to give it to him, but found his eye closed again. And she didn't know if he was asleep or just closing her out.

Nor did she know why the latter possibility settled such a big rock of regret in her belly.

SEAN WAS PRETTY DAMN close to vomiting his guts all over the place by the time Dani parked behind his rowhouse on 13th Street.

Every little bump and pothole had been like someone punching him in the chest, and that was to say nothing of what the glare of the bright summer sun and the movement of the car did to his head. Hugging a blanket to his chest that Dani had in her trunk, Sean swallowed down the sour taste of threatening upchuck. "I...think I'll...just stay right here."

"I'm sorry. Let's get you inside and you'll feel so much better."

"Not your fault, D," he managed, because the last thing he wanted was for her to feel bad for a single solitary thing, not after a twenty-four-hour period that began with him hitting her too hard and ended with her spending the night and all of today in his hospital room looking out for him. Hearing her on the phone with Mo to get him to drop her car at the hospital reminded Sean that she'd even ridden in the ambulance with him, something his brain only had a hazy recollection of. So she had absolutely nothing to apologize for. Jesus, he was the one who should be apologizing given how his trade-mark bad luck had exploded all over whatever her plans for the weekend might've been.

He pushed open his door and tried to hide his grimace at the ridiculous amount of discomfort such a little action created. For fuck sake.

"Sit still and let me help you." She rushed out of the car and around to his side, then crouched in his open doorway. "Put your arm around my shoulders."

"I can do it," he said. No way did he want her hauling his ass out of the car. Not that he doubted she was capable of it, especially knowing some of the stories from her days doing tactical critical care evac. Like how, once, her Black Hawk had been shot down, killing the co-pilot and injuring the rest of the personnel on board, including her. Dani had singlehandedly hauled all of them away from the burning wreck and administered medical care with the assistance of another medic who had a broken ankle. And when the crash finally attracted insurgents to their location, she issued covering fire so that the injured medic could continue to treat the others until backup arrived.

She hadn't told him that story. He doubted she told anyone that story. But that other medic had told people who'd told people, and it'd eventually reached him when he mentioned to a buddy that he knew her. *That* was how much of a bad-ass Daniela England was.

"Yeah, I'm sure you can do it," she said, arching a brow. "But why risk further hurting yourself? You and I both know the longer you're out of work, the more stir-crazy you're going to go."

He registered her take-charge expression as *sexy as fuck* even though his body was in no damn position to act on such a thought. Not that she'd want him to, of course. They'd been there, done that, and even though it'd been fucking awesome, he wasn't sure if she or he had backed off faster. It was entirely possible that Dani was the female version of him when it came to relationships. Hell, maybe that was part of what attracted him. "Fine," he said.

She grasped his wrist where it hung around her shoulder, gently grabbed him under his other arm, and slowly lifted him up until he could grab the top of the car door to help himself the rest of the way. "Teamwork makes the dream work," she deadpanned.

He chuckled—or started to. Except, ow. "Don't make me laugh."

"Sorry," she said, a hint of amusement in her tone.

Sean turned toward her which, given the way her arm was still around him, brought them nearly chest to chest. That was fine by him for what he had to say. "And quit apologizing to me. I'm the one who's totally imposed on your schedule."

The humor bled out of her expression. "But I owe you an apology."

He searched her black eyes and saw nothing but sincerity. "How do you figure that?"

Her shoulders dropped, but she met his gaze head on. "Because I was a bitch to you yesterday."

"I don't remember that." Not even anything remotely close to that.

Dani smirked then stepped away, and then retrieved a duffle from the back seat. "Yeah, well, your head gave the street a handshake last night so that's to be expected."

He winced at the simple fucking action of closing the car door. No wonder the doc benched his ass for the next couple of weeks. "I remember enough, D. Tell me you're not talking about what happened at fight club."

"You should've let me close that." She locked the car and started up the sidewalk that ran through his narrow backyard.

"Nice deflection."

The glare she threw him was vintage Daniela. "I'm not deflecting, asshole. I'm trying to help you."

Chuckling had him pressing his hand to his chest. "Ow, stop fucking making me laugh. And you are helping me which is why there's absolutely nothing you need to apologize for. I was the one who caused all the bullshit yesterday at WFC anyway."

"Sean—"

"No, dude, we're not relitigating this. Case closed." They reached the covered patio that led to his backdoor, and it took a stupid amount of effort to get his keys out of his jeans pocket.

"Dude." She sniggered under her breath.

"What?" he asked, nailing her with a stare after finally retrieving the keyring.

"You called me *dude*. You're like the guyest guy ever."

"Fuckin' A." He opened the door. "I'll take that as a compliment. After you."

Dani stepped inside, into the mud room surrounded on one side by a full bathroom and on the other by his laundry room. Beyond sat his family room, aka his man cave, a comfortable and cool-as-shit space that he'd given over to his love of superheroes and comic books. He hit the lights and waited for her to bust his balls.

She dropped her bag on one of the over-stuffed chairs, walked around the space, and scanned her gaze over the whole of it. Over the long black leather couch with the group of tall, stylized, red-and-white superhero portraits above. Over the black media center with all its shelves, mementos, and electronics. Over the bar in the corner, with three stools arrayed along the front and mirrored shelves holding liquor behind. All around, kick-ass 3-D art deco lights of Cap's shield, Thor's hammer, Super Man's sign, Spiderman's hand, and Iron Man's mask cast warm colors over the room.

"So...you like superheroes, then."

He crossed his arms, then quickly uncrossed them when he realized his chest was having none of it. "Shut up."

Her eyes went wide. "What? I didn't say anything."

"You didn't have to."

"Seriously, it's cool."

He gave her a look. "Don't bullshit a bullshitter."

"I'm not." She quirked a grin that was too sexy for him to get peeved. "Well maybe I'm making just a little fun, but mostly I think it's cool. You should totally have a party down here. It would be awesome." He watched as she moved about the room, ran her hand over the black marble of the bar top, and leaned in to look at a framed display of comic books. "What made you such a big fan of superheroes?"

Sean shrugged, which turned out to be another gesture his body didn't love, damnit. For a moment, he waged a mental debate, and then he came down on the side of *what the fuck* and spilled a little of his life. "I had a shit father who was also a shit cop, so the idea that there were people out there who were stronger and bigger and better, who were noble enough to do the right thing even when it wasn't popular, and whose stories gave me an escape when my house was at its worse..." He nodded. "It made me a fan for life. Also, they're kick-ass."

Daniela peered over at him then, and her gaze made him feel observed in a way that had him shifting on his feet. But then she nearly knocked him on his ass when she said, "I wish I'd known more about superheroes as a kid, then."

Did that mean she'd had a shit childhood, too? And how had they known each other for nearly five years and not known they had this in common. *Maybe it was because you're always trying to push her buttons, dickhead.*

Well. Yeah. Prolly.

He could've played it off like their words didn't hang in the air between them, weighted and important. But fuck, he was drugged, hurting, and exhausted out of his gourd. "Well, I could introduce you."

She grinned. "Introduce me how?"

In for a penny, in for a pound, even though he felt like an idiot. "Movies," he said. "You are a woman in serious need of a movie marathon."

"And you think you're the man to educate me?" She arched a playful eyebrow. And fuck she was cute—a word she'd probably rip his balls off for uttering if he was ever stupid enough to do such a thing.

"In so many things, Daniela. *So. Many.*"

She flipped him the finger, and it made him laugh. Which made him cough. Which had him clutching at his chest.

Dani was at his side in an instant. "Sit," she said, guiding him to the big couch. "I shouldn't have left you on your feet talking."

Finally, he caught his breath. "My feet might be the only thing on my body not hurting." He pulled a smirk. "Well, not the *only* thing..."

"Jesus, you're relentless." But there was no bite to it. Instead she was looking at him in this soft way—in a way no one ever looked at him.

And fuck. He liked it.

So he closed his eyes rather than chance getting used to it.

"We should get you in bed."

Bed was two floors up. "I'm good here."

"You sure?" He nodded and heard her sigh. "Well, I should at least get you some clothes to change into and some pillows to prop you up. Plus, you're due for meds again soon."

He peered up at her again, and thank God, that softness was gone. "You don't have to do all this, you know."

Her lips pressed into a tight line. "Shut up, Riddick. Now, tell me where all your shit is so I can get you set up down here."

"Gimme your phone," he said. When she hesitated, he rolled his eyes at her. "I already got your digits, D. I just want to log you into my WiFi."

She handed her cell over, her expression so skeptical it made him chuff out a laugh. He made quick work of entering the password to log her on, and then he FaceTimed himself.

"This way I can give you the guided tour of where things are while my ass is planted down here," he said, answering her Face-Time on his phone.

Her lips twisted. "That was pretty smart actually."

"Wait." He nailed her with a one-eyed stare. "Just wait. I've got a head injury and I'm seriously embracing the miracles of modern chemistry right now, but I think, just maybe, that I heard you give me a compliment."

Now she was the one rolling her eyes. She peered into her phone. "Sean?"

He looked at her through his screen, too. "Yes, Dani?"

She flipped him her middle finger right into the camera, and then dragged the tip of it over her lips as if it were lipstick.

"I think I'm aroused now," he said.

On a huff, she made for the stairs. "Just tell me where to find you some damn pillows so I can smother you with them."

CHAPTER FIVE

"You ready for that education yet?" Sean asked in a gravelly voice.

From where she sat in the oversized chair next to where he slept, Dani put down the book she'd been reading and smiled. "Hey. How'd you sleep?"

"Decent," he said, grimacing as he pushed himself into a sitting position.

"Good. No more nightmares?"

His expression went through a quick succession of emotions —confusion, something that looked a helluva lot like fear, and back to confusion again. This time with a healthy dose of guardedness. "When did I have a nightmare?"

Clearly, she needed to back way off of this topic. "At the hospital this morning. No big deal after what you went through yesterday. You hungry at all?"

When his features relaxed, she knew the topic change had been the right call. "Not really."

"You should eat something so you can take more meds." She dropped the novel onto the coffee table, a military suspense she'd found on the shelves in Sean's office.

His unbandaged eye looked to the book cover. "That's a good series."

She'd never pictured Sean being a reader before, and the image that popped into her brain of him lying in bed, shirtless—because why not shirtless?—holding a book in those big hands so he could read before going to sleep...that wasn't a half bad image. Not half bad *at all*. And since she'd found a stack of books on his bedside table, she knew her thoughts weren't just fantasy. Not that she was looking for reasons to find the sexy asshole any sexier. "Yeah? I'm enjoying it so far. Hope you don't mind."

"'Course not. The rest of them should be up there but if not I'll find 'em for you." He heaved himself off the sofa and made for the bathroom. His gait had none of his usual swagger. "Let me think about food."

"'kay."

A few minutes later, Sean cracked the door and called out. "Jesus, it looks like I took a slug while wearing a vest."

Unsurprised to hear he was bruised, Dani moved to the door and leaned against the jamb. "How bad is it?"

Sean opened the door the rest of the way, then returned to studying himself in the mirror. Holding his shirt up above the bruising gave Dani an eyeful of his muscled pecs and abdomen —and of the series of red and purple marks radiating out from the center of his chest from the blunt-force trauma of being thrown from his bike to the street. "Geez. I'm pretty sure you'd have less bruising if that was what'd happened."

He smirked. "Prolly. Always gotta be a damn overachiever."

The words had an undertone of sarcasm and humor, but they underscored for Dani something she'd never really noticed about him—how self-deprecating he was. Maybe it stood out to her now because she'd spent more time with him in the past two days than she probably ever had all at once before. Together with the revelation that he'd had a rough childhood, and it just represented that there were layers to this man she'd never given him credit for...

Sean pressed his fingers against the bruising and grimaced.

"Hey, I know what'll help. I brought an ice therapy machine. It's in my car. Be right back."

He nodded. "Turn the patio light on for yourself. Switch's by the door."

Dani retrieved her keys from her purse and slipped out the back, glad for a little space to clear her head for just a minute of all things Sean Riddick, of the realization that there was a lot more to the man than the arrogance, sarcasm, and swagger that she associated with him. Why such a realization should matter, she didn't know, because it changed nothing between them.

The night air was heavy and close, and heat lightning flashed quietly across the sky. She grabbed the unit from the trunk of her car and returned to find Sean sitting on one of the bottom steps leading to the main floor. A voicemail played out on the speaker: "Yo, Riddick. Just wanted to let you know I was thinking about you and I hope you're not too banged up. Was really sorry to hear about the accident. Shoot me a text when you're feeling up to it."

When he looked up, Dani smiled. "Your phone went off a million times. I was surprised it didn't wake you up."

He nodded. "I have a shit-ton of messages. Guys at the station."

"That's really nice."

"Yeah," he said. "Hey, you never answered my question."

Dani blinked. "About what?"

He waved a hand, indicating the superheroes surrounding them. "Watching some movies."

"I'll watch movies if you'll eat something."

His grin was immediate. The nurse in her was glad that something so small could so easily lift his spirits. "Deal."

She pointed to the unit she'd brought in from her car. "I'll set this up with some ice water and fix something to eat. What would you like?"

"Something low key."

"I did a little snooping while you were asleep to see what you had. So, maybe grilled cheese sandwiches?"

"Ooh yeah. With tomato soup. There's some in the pantry."

An unexpected pang squeezed her chest, because one of the memories she still had of her dad was of him teaching her to make a grilled cheese and then daring her to try it dunked in tomato soup—which her eight-year-old self had thought sounded gross until she tried it. Now it was a meal that always made her feel nostalgic. "Sounds good," she said.

"I can help." He pulled himself up using the bannister.

"I got it."

"D, I can microwave some damn Campbell's."

She chuckled. "Fine." She followed his slow climb up to his kitchen. That room wasn't as sleek and modern as the style of his basement but was neat and tidy with its white cabinets and counters. The main spots of color in the room came from the black coffeemaker, a red bowl filled with apples and bananas that sat on the counter, and the set of salt and pepper shakers in the shape of two superheroes' heads.

They gathered what they needed and worked side by side, her at the stove, him at the microwave. And it was weirdly...nice.

Dani used to love making meals with Anthony. The quiet intimacy of it. The way they'd move around each other, stealing kisses and touches and tastes. It'd been a lot of years since she'd last had that, and she hadn't even realized she missed it until she stood next to freaking Sean Riddick making one of her all-time favorite casual meals. How had the guy made her think of both of father and her husband with just the stupid little enthusiastic suggestion of making tomato soup?

She wasn't sure. But it threw her off kilter a little, as if she was being pulled both back in time and forward into some unknown and unknowable future that she hadn't yet decided to embrace. She flipped the sandwiches in the hot pan then peered over at Sean and found him concentrating really hard to pull the plastic seal off the top of the second microwavable soup bowl. "Need help?" she asked.

His expression morphed from one of deep concentration to frustration. "No."

Dani lowered the heat on her pan and covered it so the cheese got nice and melty. "You sure?"

His frown deepened. "No, I'm gonna make this soup can my little bitch."

A smile was just cracking on Dani's face when the plastic seal gave way so suddenly that the whole can went flying, sending soup arcing through the air and all over Sean.

He froze with his hands out at his sides. "What...the shit...."

Pressing a hand over her mouth, Dani turned off her burner and stared at the carnage that was the entire area around Riddick. A little puff of amused air escaped her effort to hold back from laughing her ass off.

He pointed at her with a hand dripping with tomato. "Don't. Say. A word." With that, he turned toward her. Orange-red liquid covered his arm, his shirt, his jeans, one of his feet. There was even a splotch of it under his good eye.

"Are you okay?" she whispered, because if she let herself do more than whisper, she was going to legit lose it.

He arched a brow. He might've looked fierce if it hadn't been for, you know, *the freaking tomato soup explosion.* "You mean, besides looking like an extra in a slasher film?" He waved a hand at himself, sending a spray of orange from his arm onto the floor.

Splat splat splat...

Which was when Dani lost it, just lost her ever-loving mind. Laughter burst out of her so hard it was nearly a cackle. She snorted with the hilarity of it, grasped her stomach to try to catch her breath, and finally crouched against the cabinet. Her cheeks hurt and her eyes were watering. She kept trying to remind him of his last words before the explosion, but every time she thought of him saying he was going to make the can his little bitch, she started laughing harder again and couldn't speak.

Sean reached for the paper towels and rolled his eyes. "Ha ha, D. Kick a man when he's down, why don't you?"

She pointed and shook her head. "You...you said...." Unable to control herself, she slumped all the way onto the floor, gasping for breath between waves of hilarity. "...l'il bitch..."

He wiped what he could off his arm and shirt, then chucked the roll at her and smirked. "While you're down there, make yourself useful."

Finally sobering up a little, Dani used the first sheet to dry and fan her face. Reaching out, she wiped up the spray of droplets that'd fallen from his arm, and then she crawled a little closer to where he stood to get the spill. Still chuckling, she wiped at the top of his bare foot. "Stand still," she managed.

"Would this be a bad time to mention that this is a nice view?" he said, amusement finally working its way into his tone.

She glared up at him, which suddenly made her aware that she was basically kneeling at his feet. "Only if you don't mind me punching your tomato-soup-covered junk." The words made her chuckle again.

With his uninjured eye, he winked. *Freaking winked.*

Dani got to her feet and sighed out the last of her humor.

"That was truly epic. Thank you. I don't think I've laughed that hard in a long time."

Sean rolled his eye. "Glad I could entertain you." He pulled at the hem of his shirt to take it off, but grimaced as he tried to pull his arms out of it.

"What are you doing?"

"I need to wash this shit and I don't want to drag tomato sauce down the steps."

"Uh, then let me help," she said. When he gave in, she gently lifted the shirt over his head, which had her realizing for the hundredth time how ripped he was and how tall he was. She'd always found marked differences in size between a man and a woman sexy, and since he had a good seven inches on her, not to mention biceps and thighs like freaking tree limbs, Sean ticked every one of her boxes in that regard. She forced her gaze away from his bruised chest to see that she'd accidentally smeared the dot of soup on his cheek. "Wait." Grinning, she reached up and wiped it away. "All better."

There was an intensity about the way he was looking at her that made her stomach take a little tumble she didn't want it to be taking, so she turned away, found the trash can under the kitchen sink, and dumped all the dirty paper towels there before turning on the faucet to wash her hands. She grabbed a clean towel to dry off and turned—

"What the fuck are you doing, Riddick?" she asked, finding Sean with his pants around his knees. The only thing he wore was a pair of dark gray boxers that fit snugly enough that they seriously did not leave much to the imagination—not that she needed to use her freaking imagination because Halloween-party hijinks of the sex-in-a-truck variety had ensued.

Sean smirked. "Don't get your panties in a twist. Ain't nothing you haven't seen before." The pants hit the floor at his ankles, and he grimaced as he reached to pick them up. "I told ya; I gotta wash this shit." He was a little pale by the time he'd finished his impromptu striptease. And the pants did in fact leave a new smear of soup on the floor that he might've trailed down the steps.

So Dani bit back the urge to give him a hard time. "Just leave the stuff there. I'll throw it in the washer for you."

He sagged against the counter. "Okay."

That he gave in so quickly told her everything she needed to know. "Stay right there. I'm going to grab you another set of clothes from your room, then we'll get you settled on the couch again and I'll bring down the food."

Upstairs, she beelined for his bedroom at the back of the house. A king-sized bed with a hunter green comforter dominated the room, which subtly smelled of Sean—all woodsy, smoky spice, like the way your clothes smelled after sitting around a campfire.

It felt strange being alone in his space like this when, before today, she'd never been to the man's house even once. Everything about the place was tasteful and understated, even if a little impersonal—well, except for the basement. She wasn't sure what she'd expected, but a part of her wouldn't have been surprised for his house to have resembled a frat, complete with foosball, sticky floors, and pin-up calendars. Which made her realize yet again how wrongly she'd judged the guy.

That realization crawled around uncomfortably inside her head. All at once, she was barraged with a quick succession of memories: Sean wanting to get her off again and again that night in his truck. The blast of arousal she'd felt when he'd pinned her down yesterday at WFC. Him telling her she was better than him. Her finding all these new layers to the man...

It was confusing as hell. And irritating, too. Because Dani didn't want to feel confused about Sean. Or, frankly, about any man.

Especially less than two weeks before Anthony's anniversary...

That thought brought a complete sucker punch of guilt that cut through all that confusion. Heaving a deep breath, she opened his dresser drawers until she found a T-shirt and a pair of worn-soft sweatpants that she thought might be more comfortable than jeans. Downstairs again, she found him standing, arms braced against the counter, head sagging, his back to her.

For just a moment, the picture he made there stole her breath. His body was a freaking masculine work of art. The broad, muscled back. The tight ass. The tattoos stretched stark across his skin.

How she could even notice such things with that guilt sloshing around inside her, she didn't know. But it sure as heck didn't make her feel great about herself, that was for sure.

She was here as a nurse, and maybe a bit as his friend—but certainly not as his lover. Which had her looking past his body to see that his effort to help make dinner had drained him of whatever energy sleeping had provided. "Hey," she said. "Here are some clean clothes."

He turned slowly, though not slow enough to fully remove the exhaustion from his face before he looked at her. "Thanks."

She stood in front of him. "Lean back against the counter and lift one leg at a time."

He reached for the pants. "I got it."

Dani shot him a look. "Conserve your energy, Riddick. This is going to be a marathon for you over the next week or two. Accept all the help you can get."

On a sigh, he rested his hips against the counter and did what she said, allowing her to slide one pants leg and then the other over his feet and onto his calves. Sean took over from there. "I don't like needing help."

Well, she couldn't blame him for that. "I get it. I don't either. But sometimes we all need it, you know?"

"Yeah," he said as she put the shirt over his head.

"Besides, would you rather have Mo or Billy helping you dress, or me?"

He smirked. "Is *un*dressing an option here? 'Cause if so, I'd rather have you do that."

"Oh, my God," she said with a groan. The last thing she needed was him flirting with her. "You are flippin' relentless."

He chuffed out a little laugh. "I gotta be me. Ain't no one else I can be."

"All right, well, take all of that—" She waved a hand in his general direction. "—and go sit your ass down. Dinner's about to be served, and then you owe me some movies."

Sean gave a single nod and turned toward the stairs.

Which was the first time Dani saw the writing on the back of his shirt.

Engine Company 11
Truck Company 6
Finding 'em hot
Leaving 'em wet

"Even your freaking shirts are relentless," she called.

He stopped, looked down at himself, and then peered over his shoulder, a spark of Sean's normal arrogance and challenge in those dark eyes. "Truth in advertising, D. That's all it is. Not that I need to tell you."

Dani gawped. Then glared. Then shook her head. "I don't have any damn idea what you're talking about, Riddick." Even though, hell yeah, she remembered exactly what he'd wrung out of her body. And how many times.

He sniggered. "Play it that way if you want to," he called as he started down the steps again. "But we both know that ain't true."

Damn him. He was right. But no good would come of admitting it, not when she intended for it to never happen again.

AN HOUR LATER, they were on the couch together, dinner dishes discarded on the coffee table, the ice machine strapped to his chest, and laughing their asses off.

Well, she sure was. He was more trying to laugh on the inside so that his chest would stop screaming at him. For fuck's sake.

At least this time, Sean wasn't the butt of the joke.

Dani was fucking loving 'Deadpool', and that fact delighted Sean to no end. She'd already been grinning as the credits rolled at the top of the movie, which he appreciated because they were fuckin' funny. And then she'd chuckled at the first fourth-wall break right at the beginning, where Deadpool talks to the audience about fondling Wolverine's balls. And then she'd sat wide-eyed at the over-the-top nature of the first action sequence, grinned at the "some of the best love stories start with a murder" line which she remembered him saying at the hospital, and finally erupted in full-out belly laughter when Wade bit Vanessa with his plastic vampire teeth while giving her oral sex.

All of which made Sean glad he'd given in to her demand to watch 'Deadpool' first even though he'd tried to explain the whole order of the Marvel universe thing. She just hadn't cared that 'Deadpool' was nowhere near the beginning. And it didn't matter to him just then either, because she was digging something he loved.

And Sean couldn't get enough of it.

"Stop watching my reactions," she'd finally said after the montage of sex scenes ended.

"I'm not watching you," he lied. Because he was definitely watching her reactions. And liking them. And liking looking at her in this unhurried way that he never had with her any other time.

Damn, she was fuckin' beautiful. The long glossy dark hair. The almost regal shape of her face, with its high cheekbones, wide eyes, and bow-shaped mouth. Her easy smile and laughter.

Her being gorgeous was not a news flash, of course, because Sean had clocked that from the first second he'd seen her at Warrior Fight Club almost five years ago. But admiring that beauty as she sat in his house, on his couch, watching 'Deadpool' with him and loving it? That was something way the hell else.

He liked it a stupid lot.

As if that mattered. He knew it didn't. He was well aware that Daniela England was sitting in his house and on his couch while laughing at his movie only because his ass needed caring for in the wake of getting up-close-and-personal with a box truck. She was here out of a sense of duty, out of being the kind of person who did right by other people. *Not* for any other reason. And certainly not because she cared what he thought about her.

Words were tumbling out of his mouth before he'd made the conscious decision to spill them. "You don't have to stay, you know."

Dani's gaze whipped toward him, her brows cranked down. "What the fuck, Riddick? I'm watching 'Deadpool' here. You can't be all 'you're a woman in serious need of a movie marathon' and then kick me out halfway through the first flick."

With a little chuckle he held up his hands. "Wasn't trying to kick you out, D. Stay as long as you like. Just didn't want you to feel, I don't know, stuck here. I got it from here."

"First of all, Mr. Campbell's Soup Man, you're only, like, thirty hours out of getting your butt run over. Second, I don't feel stuck here. I'm happy to help. Now can we get back to seeing if Wade is going to catch Francis and rescue Vanessa or what?"

He smiled despite the soup-related dig. "My Deadpool is your Deadpool."

They watched the rest of the movie in silence—well, *not talking*. Dani's amusement kept it from being anything but silent. Not that Sean was complaining.

And then, finally, Vanessa and Wade were together again, facing each other, as Vanessa saw how much Wade's appearance had changed for the first time. Dani wore a perma-grin as the scene unfolded. And then Vanessa said a line that was easily one of the best movie lines of all time:

"After a brief adjustment period and a bunch of drinks, it's a face...I'd be happy to sit on."

Laughter erupted out of Dani, and she sat rapt through the end of the movie until the credits finally rolled. "Oh my God, Sean, *that* was epic." She turned toward him, smiling and recounting some of her favorite lines. Enthusiastic as all hell.

A little bit blown away, he nodded and joked in all the right places. It was just that Dani was always such a bad-ass bullbuster that he wasn't sure he'd ever seen this funny, laid-back side of her, the one open to his kind of stupid humor. Was it possible that, with all his sarcasm and snark, he'd never given her the chance to show him that side of herself?

And then Dani suggested they watch 'Deadpool 2'.

Even though it was after ten, he was wasted, and his eye was aching like a motherfucker, Sean was happy to oblige. Because

Dani wasn't interested in this out of obligation or to humor him. She was truly into this.

Which had one of Sean's favorite lines going through his head: *"Your crazy matches my crazy. Big time."*

Not that he was sharing that with her.

Because he didn't even know the point of thinking it himself.

CHAPTER SIX

THE FIRST THING Dani knew was the kink in her neck. The second thing was that her pillow was really hard. The third was that she was not in her own bed.

She flew into a sitting position, her heart taking sudden flight. Hitting the home button on her cell phone revealed that it was four in the morning.

Not late. Okay, not late. Calm down.

Heaving a deep breath, she shook off the haze of sleep and peered to her left, to Sean, who was sound asleep despite her freak-out. He was mostly sitting upright, pillows piled high against his far side to offer support. A sliver of light spilled over his sleeping face from the bathroom, where the light had been left on behind a mostly closed door. The only sound in the room was the soft *whirr* of the ice machine.

Awareness finally returned. They'd been watching movies. And, oh, hell, 'Deadpool' was a freaking riot. It was so totally Riddick's brand of snarky, innuendo-laden, off-color humor, though she couldn't deny that she'd laughed more at those two movies than she had in a long time. So clearly it was her humor, too. Which was interesting to her.

Obviously, she and Sean had things in common—prior military, WFC members, a shared group of friends. Typically, all that was overshadowed for her by how much he tended to get on her last nerve. Yet, she'd been the one to push for watching 'Deadpool 2'.

But after the mostly sleepless night she'd had at the hospital, her eyes had grown so heavy that she'd stretched out on her side of the couch... She didn't remember falling asleep.

And certainly not against Sean's thigh.

The light from her phone illuminated something on the floor beside her, and she reached down to find that a blanket had puddled there. The thing was, Dani hadn't had a blanket when she'd laid down, which meant...Sean had covered her.

Which was something Anthony always used to do.

Dani would fall asleep watching TV or reading a book, and he would grab the blanket off the back of the couch and cover her up. Waking up with the blanket on her always made her smile. Proof that Anthony was thinking of her and taking care of her, even when she didn't know it.

With the comparison sitting uncomfortably in Dani's gut, she got up and closed herself inside the bathroom. She couldn't quite meet her own gaze in the mirror, which was maybe ridiculous since she hadn't done anything to feel guilty about. Still felt guilty all the same, though.

But why in the world would *Sean* make her feel guilty?

Sure, they'd hooked up that one time, but that wasn't why she was here now. And anyway, she was too old—and her field of fucks-to-give was too barren—to feel guilty over fulfilling a perfectly natural urge from time to time. Having sex didn't make her feel guilty, because sex was just...sex. It didn't mean that there was a relationship or a commitment or emotion. And Sean hadn't been her first partner after Anthony.

She used the toilet, grimaced at how loud flushing sounded

against the stillness of the night, then washed her hands. Finally, she looked at herself in the mirror.

Out of nowhere, a knot filled her throat and threatening tears stung the backs of her eyes.

She was lonely. God, she was so freaking lonely.

That's what Sean covering her and leaving a light on for her made her feel. Because the last person who'd done things like that for her was her dead husband.

"No," she whispered to herself. "*No.*" Dani shook her head, fisted her hands, and clenched her eyes—all to push those tears back. Tears helped exactly nothing. You couldn't see anything while your eyes were blurred with tears—her granny taught her that. Besides, Dani had no cause to throw herself a pity party. She had a good life—friends, a fantastic job, a nice apartment, and money in the bank. She wasn't looking for a relationship. She wasn't particularly interested in having kids. This was the life she'd purposely created after Anthony died. And lots of other people she'd cared about were gone and no longer had any kind of life at all. She should be grateful.

Right. And she was. So.

She forced a deep, cleansing breath, pushing the last of the unusual emotions away.

Glancing at her phone told her it was now almost four thirty. She had to be at the hospital at seven and debated just going in early. The likelihood of falling back to sleep at this rate seemed slim. But it also felt weird to sneak out on Sean in the middle of the night as if she were doing some kind of walk of shame.

Whatever she decided, she was itching for a shower and a fresh set of clothes she hadn't been wearing for going on thirty-six hours. She'd brought a set of scrubs to sleep in but had fallen asleep before changing. At least that left her clean clothes for work....

Which settled it. She was getting a shower. And if Sean didn't wake up on his own by six, she'd leave him a note and remind him that Billy would be over some time in the morning. It was a plan—a plan that just required retrieving her duffle bag from the family room.

She turned off the bathroom light so opening the door wouldn't shine light over the basement, and then tiptoed out into the hallway. Her bag should be right over—

"You okay, D?" Sean's voice was a low rumble in the dark.

"Yeah. Shit, I'm sorry. I was trying not to wake you up."

"You didn't. A hazard of sleeping a lot of nights at the firehouse is always having one ear tuned to what's happening around you whether you're asleep or not."

"You need anything?" she asked, finding her bag where she'd left it next to one of the chairs.

He didn't respond long enough that she thought he hadn't heard her, but then he finally murmured, "No. I'm good."

Something in his tone didn't sound good. "Sure?"

"Yeah."

"Why don't I get you some meds? It's been at least six hours."

"Nah, it's bearable."

She moved closer, as if proximity would make deciphering him easier. "You don't need to tough this out, especially not so soon. If you're feeling pain, you should take the meds. The more you can stay ahead of the pain the better it'll be."

"Watch your eyes." It was the only warning he gave before he turned on the lamp beside him.

Dani blinked against the brightness, but her eyes adjusted quickly after being in the bathroom. "Hey," she said.

"Hey." He peered up at her with an expression that was way...softer or more open, maybe, than anything she'd ever seen him wear before.

And she didn't know how to read it.

"Will you help me get this off?" he tugged at the rectangular pad Velcroed around his chest through which the ice water flowed.

"Yeah. Did it help?" she asked as she began removing the straps that held the plastic pad in place.

He turned a little so she could better reach his back. "I think it did. But I guess I'll take some more meds, too. Don't really like needing them."

"I get it. But it's only been two days. Use the ice machine as much as you want though, just don't try to carry it yourself. I've got a whole line-up of help coming this week, starting with Billy sometime this morning. There." She moved the pad, straps, and cooler unit aside.

"Thanks for doing all this, D."

"You're welcome."

How unusual was it for the two of them to have an exchange marked by sincerity instead of sarcasm? It was...weird. Very adult of them, but weird.

"I'll get your meds and then I'm going to hop in the shower if that's okay. I have to be at the hospital by seven, so I'm just going to head in early."

"My shower is your shower."

She smiled, remembering him saying the same thing about 'Deadpool' last night. "Thanks. I'll check in with you to see how you're doing, okay? My next day off is Thursday, so I'll be back then."

Sean peered up at her and shook his head. "You don't have to do that."

"What, are you kidding? I know I don't have to, but you promised me an education and I want more Marvel." She wasn't just saying that either. The idea of coming back...surprisingly wasn't something she felt obligated to do. In fact, she hadn't felt obligated to do any of this. Really, it'd never been a question to her. She'd just done it—the ambulance, the night at the hospital, spending yesterday with him.

His grin was immediate. "Yeah? All right then. It's a plan."

An hour later, Dani was on her way to University Hospital, a long shift in front of her. But something about her conversation with Sean had chased all those messy middle-of-the-night emotions far, far away, leaving her simply feeling ready to tackle her day.

THE KNOCK at the back door came a little before eleven.

Sean turned off the TV from the whole lotta nothing he'd been watching, heaved his ass off the couch, and found Billy waiting, plastic container in hand.

"There's the man," Billy said. "How the hell are ya?"

"Hey, B. Come on in."

The button-down shirt tucked into a pair of black dress pants clearly meant Billy had taken time out of his workday to stop by. The guy held out the container. "From Shayna, who's upset she couldn't get away from work today. She promises to come see you soon. And she made you these."

"Shit, she didn't have to do anything," Sean said, even more touched after he removed the lid to find homemade Snickerdoodles, his favorite cookie. "But I'm fuckin' glad she did. Breakfast!" He took a bite of one and soft, chewy, cinnamony goodness exploded on his tongue.

"Right? That's what I said when she questioned the three I ate this morning."

Sean gestured to the couch. "Never question Snickerdoodles. That's all I'm saying." As they sat, he tried like hell to keep from showing that the shoulda-been-nothing movement took effort. Anything that used his abs or pecs was a no-go.

"How are you feeling, seriously?" Billy asked, snagging a cookie for himself.

Sean pushed the bowl in between them, apparently having failed at acting like everything was normal if Billy's question was any guide. "I'm fuckin' fine. Shitty, but fine."

Billy nodded. "As someone who's dealt with pain, I'm telling you that you just need to give in to healing. You can't will it away. You can't ignore it away. And doing things you shouldn't do will just make it hurt longer."

Sean glanced at the mottled skin just barely visible on the side of Billy's neck—burns scars from an ambush on his Army Ranger unit that had led to B's medical discharge and months of recovery. If anybody had the creds to give that advice, it was Billy Parrish. "I hear ya. Problem is I'm gonna go stir crazy."

"I get it," Billy said. "Pretend you're on vacation and watch some movies or binge some Netflix."

"I haven't taken a single vacation since the navy," Sean said, even as the mention of movies made his thoughts stray to Dani. Or, more particularly, to the fact that Sean's brain had unhelpfully conjured up an image of Dani naked in the very same shower he'd been using. He'd gotten so hard he'd given in to jacking himself. Because he was apparently a horny bastard even while in pain. But at least that part of him still worked.

"Then you're overdue." Billy grabbed two more cookies. "Or maybe get a hobby."

Sean arched a brow at the suggestion and the cookies. "How many of these do you have at your own house, asshole?"

Smirking, Billy shrugged. "A lot. Chocolate chip, too. Shayna's awesome like that."

"That's a fact. So fuckin' pace yourself on my stash." Sean took another and just barely resisted hugging the bowl to his chest and calling it *his precious*. (Yeah, he was a 'Lord of the Rings' fan too. Fuckin' sue him.)

Chuckling, Billy asked, "So, since you're still alive, I take it you and Dani didn't kill each other?"

"No, man, it was cool," Sean said nonchalantly.

His friend's brows lifted. "Really? I mean, that's great. Just, you know, two days ago you were yelling at each other at WFC."

"We didn't yell," he said, feeling inexplicably defensive. Of what'd happened that day, which he still felt bad about. And of Dani.

"Okay, you were talking vigorously."

Sean shrugged, then grimaced as pain followed the gesture. "Whatever. It was good. She was a huge help and we watched 'Deadpool'. And speaking of help, she brought me this ice therapy machine. Would you mind filling it with fresh ice and water? I'd rather use the ice than keep taking the pain pills." He asked because he needed help with that. But he'd also asked to change the subject from Dani. He felt oddly private about the unusually easy-going time he and D had spent together and didn't really want to share it or have people speculating about it.

"Yeah, of course."

They made their way up to the kitchen, Billy a lot faster than Sean. "You have time for some lunch?" Sean asked when he'd finally lumbered to the top of the steps.

"Yeah, I'm free until about twelve thirty. Then I have a few security clearance interviews to do." As a private investigator, Billy's cases ranged from clearance to fraud to infidelity investigations. He'd even handled a few missing persons cases.

"I can order a pizza from the place down the street or I got cold cuts."

Billy emptied the lukewarm water from the cooler unit into

the sink. "Don't go to any trouble. Sandwiches are great. In fact, maybe I should make them?"

"Nah, man, sandwiches I can handle." At least he hoped he could. Though, he'd thought he could handle a soup can, too. The memory had him grudgingly smiling to himself. He managed to assemble everything he needed, including the last of the hoagie rolls he'd bought, and then he opened one of the cabinets and reached up for some plates. A ripping sensation stole his breath.

"Shit, dude," Billy said, catching the plates before Sean dropped them. "I think stretching and handling any sort of weight overhead are off limits for a few more days."

Sean bit back a complaint, because the man standing next to him had survived *way* worse. "Yeah." He half-gasped out the word, unhappily admitting that the doc had been right to say Sean needed to take medical leave from work. Hand clutching where pain still seized his chest, he imagined trying to stretch the line or swing an ax. And...nope. Right now, he'd be a liability to his brothers in his company. Which fuckin' sucked. When he could, he sighed. "For a split second I forget I shouldn't do something until I do it."

"Happens to me all the time. Damn burn scars are inelastic as hell."

Sean gave him a long glance, because he'd never heard him talk about his injuries so casually. Or really, like, at all. Probably Shayna's influence, if Sean had to guess. Because Billy had been a changed man since he and Shayna had gotten together the night of the apartment explosion that Sean and Shay had worked together, him fighting the fire, her photographing it. Billy was lighter somehow. Laughed more freely. Rarely appeared like a man with the weight of the world on his shoulders. All of which made Sean like and respect Shayna more than he already did. She was good people—the best.

"I'll fill this with fresh ice after we eat," Billy said, setting the machine aside.

Nodding, Sean picked up the plates laden with overstuffed sandwiches and barbecue chips. "This way."

Billy swiped them out of his hands. "Dude. No carrying for you."

"They're plates."

"Plates that just kicked your ass two minutes ago."

"I don't like you," Sean groused.

Billy grinned. "Right back atcha."

They settled around the dining room table Sean rarely used in part because he so infrequently had people at the house. No particular reason, except that, with all the overtime shifts he pulled, he didn't really spend that much non-sleeping time here himself.

Over ham and cheese sandwiches, they talked about Billy's cases, Sean's call with the station chief that morning to figure out what he needed to do to take leave, and how the chief was sorry for what'd happened but thought Sean deserved the time off after the hours he always put in. Finally, they landed on Warrior Fight Club.

One more thing Sean was already regretting missing. WFC was part of what kept him level and helped him blow off steam. No work *and* no fight club? That was going to be a killer combination that left him with too much free time—and free head space—on his hands. "It's gonna suck missing it," Sean said. "But I guess this is one more way I'm benched for a few weeks."

"I can't go to WFC this week either. Hoping to make dinner, though," Billy said around a bite of chips.

"Working?"

"Actually, no. I'm going to a Nat's game with my Little." When Sean frowned, Billy continued. "You know, Big Brothers/Big Sisters. I signed up to be a Big and got matched about a month ago. My Little's name is Dante. He's twelve."

"That's...pretty damn cool. Is this because of those features Shayna worked on?" She and another reporter had published a fantastic series of stories on different aspects of the program last fall and winter.

"Yeah," Billy said. "She learned that Big Brothers are in especially high demand. They're always looking for men to be mentors, and there's always a waitlist of boys waiting to be matched." He looked down and shrugged. "I guess I was wanting to be a part of something, I don't know, bigger than just my job."

The sentiment hit Sean in his already-hurting chest. He got that feeling even though he didn't know what to do with it. "Wow. So what do you and Dante do together?" Sean asked.

"We mostly just hang out. The baseball game is a special sponsored event for Bigs and Littles. Usually, we play games at my house or take my neighbor's dog for a walk or go have a meal. I try to take my cues from him, you know?"

"That's really awesome of you, B."

He shrugged. "Honestly, I dig spending time with him, so it's not just for him." Billy eyeballed Sean for a long minute. "You know, you should check it out. You could take your Little to meet the guys at the firehouse and show him the ropes there. Man, kids would dig that."

They often had school groups visit the firehouse during the day, so Sean knew firsthand how much kids enjoyed seeing the trucks and hearing the sirens and call tones. Not to mention visiting the station cat, Winston, who'd just sort of arrived one day and stayed, like he'd adopted them instead of the other way around.

"Yeah? Huh. I never thought of something like that," Sean

said, wondering if he'd be any good at it. What did he know about spending time with kids?

"I hadn't either," Billy said, wiping his mouth and checking the time on his phone. "Shit, I gotta go in about fifteen."

Feeling a little more fortified by the food, Sean dropped his napkin on his plate. "Thanks for coming by. Really."

"You know my schedule has some flexibility, so if you need me, hit me up." Billy carried their dishes to the sink and insisted on loading them into the dishwasher and wiping down the counter despite Sean's assurances that he could take care of it later. Then the guy filled the ice unit and asked, "Now, how do you use this thing?"

A few minutes later, Sean was sitting on the couch downstairs and strapped back into the machine, courtesy of Billy and a whole lot of trying not to laugh as he struggled with the stickiness of the Velcro straps. They said their good-byes and B saw his way out, and then Sean was back to flipping channels on the idiot box.

Not that anything held his interest, so for a while he shot off messages to the guys at the station who'd texted or left voicemails. He hated the reason for all the attention, but he couldn't deny that it felt good to be thought of by so many people. The firehouse and his friends at WFC were like family, especially since he had none of his own—or at least none who cared.

When he'd sent the last of his replies, he stared at the old movie that he hadn't really been watching. His attention strayed...to the wall-mounted art deco lights of Captain America and Thor that hung on either side of the television. Sean's gaze tracked next to his comic book collection. And the collectible figures arrayed on a shelf.

A kid would like this place.

Man, if he'd had a friend with a set-up like this when he'd

been twelve, he would've offered to sell body parts to move in forever and never have to go home again.

Huh.

On a grimace, he reached for his laptop on the coffee table. Booted it up. Opened a search window.

Just out of curiosity, he typed in, *what does it take to become a big brother*

Even though, as a workaholic in a high-risk job who carried some serious baggage he mostly tried to ignore, he was pretty sure he didn't qualify to be anybody's role model.

Still, he started reading. What else did he have to do?

CHAPTER SEVEN

IT WAS ENTIRELY possible that Sean was putting too much time and attention into preparing for Dani's Avengers education. He placed an online grocery order to restock his pantry. Rush-ordered his favorite caramel and cheese popcorns. And, in between a steady stream of get-well and funny-meme texts from the guys at the station and his friends at WFC, Sean had begun strategizing over the best viewing order.

There were multiple ways to approach this. In order of movie release was the most obvious, of course, which put 'Iron-man' first. But that movie actually came chronologically later in the universe, which argued for 'Captain America'—which largely took place in the 1940s—and a newer movie, 'Captain Marvel'—which mostly occurred in the 1990s, to be one and two. Then 'Ironman' would fit in after that.

Sean nodded to himself as he plugged this information into a spreadsheet until, finally, he'd determined the perfect thematic viewing order for all twenty-plus existing movies in the universe.

Not that they were watching them all on Thursday, of course, but maybe they'd get through the first couple, anyway.

Which had Sean picking up his cell and firing off a text Dani's way. *What time are you coming tomorrow—*

He deleted that and started again. *You still coming by tomorrow?* Better. He didn't want to assume. He hit *Send.*

An hour was a long-ass time when you weren't otherwise occupied, and that was how long it took for Dani to reply: *Was planning on it. That still okay?*

He grinned at his phone. *Hell yes. Just wondered what time and how long you were thinking of staying so I can make a plan.*

We need a plan?

What the shit? Of course we need a plan. I made a spreadsheet. He frowned. Maybe he should've kept the spreadsheet to himself. Because Dani likely had no idea there were so many movies to watch, and he couldn't imagine her being game for his level of fanaticism.

...

Those three dots were her only reply. Sean chuckled as his thumbs flew. *Just trust me.*

FAMOUS LAST WORDS

That had him laughing out loud, which had him grasping his chest. Leave it to Daniela England to bust his balls via text. His cell *dinged* another incoming message.

Fine. I'll be there around ten and I have the whole day off so I'm happy to help with anything you need. Want me to bring some groceries over?

He was well aware that it represented some seriously low expectations, but he was proud of himself for being able to say: *Got it covered. See you then.*

After that, Sean was back to a whole lotta nothing to do. He didn't even have his bike to work on, which had been his usual go-to when idle hands threatened to leave him with too much time to think about the past and the long list of mistakes he'd made—and about how those mistakes had gotten others hurt.

Too much time to think about why he was here when others weren't—others who maybe deserved to survive more than he did.

Sean shook his head and forced the thoughts away. No. No way. He wasn't gonna sit and spin on those kinds of thoughts. Not today, Satan.

There was at least one thing bike-related he could do, so he called his insurance company to determine the process for the claim regarding his bike. The good news was that the insurance company was available to send an adjuster to evaluate his bike's condition this week. The bad news was that talking to his insurance agent was his idea of a good time these days.

For fuck's sake.

Luckily, Mo texted a little before five to save him from boredom and overthinking. *You up for chili dogs with me, Billy, and Shayna? I can swing by and pick you up.*

Hell yes.

Mo was there by six, and they made it the short distance to Ben's Chili Bowl fifteen minutes later. Billy and Shayna were inside and had grabbed them a table.

When she saw Sean, Shayna rose to her feet in an instant, her bright blue eyes filled with excitement to see him, and her arms reaching for a hug—before she stopped short. "Oh, I don't know if I should hug you."

"Yeah, o'course," he managed, moved by her affection for him. And just a little uncomfortable as her arms came gently around him. Sean was weird about hugs, maybe because he'd rarely had them in his life. His mother had died when he was young enough that he didn't have many first-hand memories of her. His father was an abusive asshole. While he'd had plenty of sex, a decade in the navy plus nearly five years of pulling every extra shift he could at the station hadn't left him much time for relationships. So hugs just felt...weird to him. Foreign.

Soon their table was piled high with chili dogs, half smokes, and amazing fries. "How are you feeling?" Shayna asked him.

All eyes turned to him. "My chest is starting to feel a little better today. I can take deeper breaths easier, anyway."

"That sounds like good news," Mo said from where he sat beside Sean. "How long before you can get back to work?"

"Chief gave me four weeks of leave. I don't know if I'll need that long. A lot depends on my vision clearing up." A feeling of dread stalked around in his chest. What if it didn't? Jesus, he didn't know what he'd do if it didn't.

Billy glanced at the eye shield covering Sean's injury. "When will you know more about your eye?"

His stomach tossed a little around the bites of chili dog in his gut. "I have an appointment with the specialist on Friday. They told me not to take the shield off before then, but it's been fucking tempting." It was true. He'd been itching to see if his vision was any clearer than it'd been the day he'd been discharged. So much depended on it.

"Shit," Billy said. "I've got back-to-back meetings all day on Friday or I'd offer to go with you."

Sean appreciated the thought. "Don't worry about it, but thanks. What's going on with you guys?" he asked, hoping to shift the attention off him and his damn injuries.

"Actually, that's part of why I was hoping we could all get together tonight," Mo said in his deep voice. "Because I have news."

"Oh, yeah? What's up, man?" Sean asked.

"I've decided I'm tired of jumping from contract gig to contract gig. A year here. Six months there. Always being in job-hunting mode. Never really putting down roots or feeling like I'm part of something meaningful." Mo shook his head. Since he'd retired from the Army Rangers almost eight years before, he'd been working variously for the feds or defense contractors, but this past stretch of months he'd been seeming less satisfied with it.

Billy dunked his fries in ketchup. "We've talked about it many times. You know I feel you on all of that."

Mo nodded. "I'm gonna open my own security services company. Personal security for individuals, executives, celebrities, and diplomats; secure transportation, security consulting, and private investigation. We'll expand services as we bring on personnel. Guys coming out of the Spec Ops communities often face challenges in finding jobs that match their skill sets, so I'm prioritizing hiring veterans." He laid a portfolio on the table and his gaze swung to Billy. "And I'm putting together a small group of partners to help me get this thing off the ground."

Billy's dark-eyed gaze lifted from the folder to Mo's face. His brows went way up. "Partners."

"Mmhmm. I was hoping you might be open to joining me." He slid the papers closer. "So this is for you. Read it over. Think about it. No pressure."

"This is seriously cool, Mo," Sean said, grinning. "Congratulations. I can't wait to see this come together for you." They bumped fists.

"Thanks. I'm pretty fucking hyped about it." Sean could tell, because Mo hadn't seemed this relaxed in months.

"Billy?" Shayna said, peering at the sorta shell-shocked man sitting next to her.

He blinked and looked at her. She gave him a smile and a tiny nod. And that was all it took for Billy to turn back to Mo and say one word. "Yes." He picked up the portfolio. "Of course, I'll read it. But there's not going to be anything in these pages that changes my answer. The rest we can work out." The two men hadn't served together, but they'd both been Army Rangers, so this didn't surprise Sean at all.

Now Mo was full-on grinning. "You're in?"

"I'm in," Billy said. They shook hands across the table, and then everyone was laughing and smiling.

"Damn, I'm glad to be able to say I was there from the start," Sean said, truly happy for his friends. "And if you ever need a smoke-breathing hose dragger, I might consider hiring myself out. For the right price." He winked.

Mo chuckled. "I'm sure we'll have plenty of fires to put out, Riddick, but hopefully none of them will be of the actual-flame variety. We do, though, and you're our man."

"Boom. Done," Sean said, hoping he would in fact get to return to his job. Unlike Mo, he already had his dream job, so long as his injury didn't prevent him from meeting the vision requirements.

And, sonofabitch, that was entirely out of his hands.

But there was nothing he could do about that but wait. So, fine. In the meantime, he could get out of his head and celebrate something good happening to his friends, because it sometimes seemed in this world like good things didn't happen often enough to good people. And he'd look forward to his movie marathon with Dani.

Yeah, he was looking forward to that a stupid lot.

CHAPTER EIGHT

Dani felt oddly nervous, and it was freaking ridiculous.

It was just that this was the first time she'd gone to Sean's house on what was more or less a purely social call, and even though the basic purpose was to help him out and keep him company, his issues were no longer acute the way they'd been nearly a week before. It wasn't that she wasn't looking forward to watching movies with him, because she was. It was just that, as she approached his back door, she felt like less of a nurse and more of a friend.

Or whatever they were.

Even that offhand thought felt disingenuous after being thrown together after his accident.

She knocked. The door swung open.

Sean looked...so much better. That mischievous light was back in his eyes—well, the one not covered by the taped shield of course. His color was better. He stood taller, his big body filling almost the whole doorway.

Standing there in a pair of worn jeans and a white T-shirt that set off the tan on his muscular arms, he was back to being fucking hot. And he was well enough that she didn't have to feel like a creeper for noticing.

"You comin' in?" he asked, amusement in his tone.

"Uh, yeah, of course. Thanks." She moved into his family room and watched as he closed the door behind her. "You look better."

"Starting to feel human again. My chest actually looks worse, though." He helpfully lifted his shirt to reveal that the bruising had in fact spread. But bruises often appeared worse before they got better.

For just a split second, Dani had this stray thought: *Maybe it would feel even better if I licked it.* The hard pads of his pecs. The ridges of his abdomen. For starters.

Ack. What the heck was wrong with her?

He dropped his shirt and continued as if she wasn't standing there imagining seriously violating his personal space, to put it mildly. "But I'm not coughing quite as much and I can do more than I could."

She nodded. "Good. That's good." Needing to look at something besides his climbable body—*oh, great, Dani, first he's lickable, now he's climbable*—she turned towards the couch and found that he'd laid out a spread on the coffee table. Popcorn, pretzels, cookies, drinks.

"Yeah, so, I got us some snacks," he said, running a hand over his dark hair. Was he nervous? He sounded a little nervous. Or maybe she was projecting? Gah, what was even happening here? "Uh, but if there's something else you might want—"

"No, this looks great, Sean. I would've helped you bring all this down, though. You have to be careful not to overdo it."

"I didn't. I promise. I saved the ice machine for you, if you don't mind. But the rest was no problem."

"Of course." She dropped her purse onto the chair and grabbed a few pieces of cheese popcorn and a few pieces of caramel. "Do you ever eat these together?" she asked, popping one of each into her mouth. "It seems like it should be weird, but it's really good."

Sean blinked and then a slow smile grew on his face. "That's how I eat them. I only put them in separate bowls for you."

She grinned. "Great minds."

"Right?" He nodded. "Also, you just called my mind great, for the record. I think we need to mark this occasion."

Dani rolled her eyes. "Don't make me change my opinion."

He chuckled. She grinned. *Gah why does this feel like a date?!*

Luckily, things felt more normal by the time she got him hooked up to the ice machine and he queued up the movie. "'Captain America' is first."

"Why is that?" she asked. "Since you mentioned having a spreadsheet and all." She smirked at him, even though their text exchange the day before had made her smile. And then she'd purposely frowned because why was she smiling at texts from Sean Riddick? But *then* someone had caught her smiling and teased her about whether she had a secret sexting partner and that'd made her inexplicably blush. Damnit. And she wasn't even normally a blusher!

"It occurs chronologically earliest, in the 1940s."

"Okay. Just how many movies are there in this world?" She eyed his laptop sitting open on the end table.

Sean blanked his expression, like he was purposely suppressing a reaction. "Uh, it's better if you just go with the flow here."

"How many?"

"Really—"

"Five?"

He coughed on a piece of popcorn.

"Ten?"

Clearing his throat, he said, "It's a *robust* universe, okay? Leave it at that."

"Fifteen?" She'd originally asked out of curiosity, but now she was having fun trying to make him react. Which was why she launched a surprise attack in reaching across his lap to grab his computer. Her fingers had just grasped at the corner of it when Sean's arms banded around her mid-section—one hand on her hip and the other wrapping under her and landing on her side—and pulled her back.

"What do you think you're doing, woman?"

His arms were so freaking strong, and God his hands were big where they held her tight. One arm brushed the underside of her breast and the other gripped her hip, and both were freaking arousing. "I was seeing how many movies there are. And this hold is unfair because I can't fight you off without hurting you."

Grinning, he held her tighter, forcing her to brace her hands on his thigh. "Yes, be very careful, Daniela. I'm super fragile over here. You wouldn't want to hurt me."

She glared at him.

But he was grinning like an idiot. And his good humor was freaking appealing. Which she was sure had nothing to do with the way he was holding her and how close their bodies were. It would be such a little thing to turn into him, to straddle him, and to make this day about something entirely else...

"You want to punch me right now, don't you?"

"Very much." She bit the words out more sternly than she'd intended, mostly because she was so thrown off guard by the direction of her own thoughts. If only her brain didn't know how freaking good this man was at scratching an itch.

He winked at her. "Good. You're channeling some serious Peggy Carter right now. That's perfect. That fighting spirit will put you in good stead for 'Captain America'."

"Who's Peggy Carter?"

Sean let her go, and she sat back in her own spot. "That question kills me. Literally, I might die sitting here. So let's get started and you'll see. Also, if you cross the demilitarized zone again"—he indicated the space in between them—"I won't be held responsible for my actions." He arched a brow. One that held a hint of something beyond humor.

It held a promise.

Dani was almost tempted to test it. Consequences be damned.

Instead, she rolled her eyes, but the gesture was a lie. She was neither annoyed nor unaffected. Oh, no, the heat in her body indicated she was very much affected by the good-guy, playful, nerdy, super-hero-loving version of Sean Riddick. The one who was also freaking hot. And the one who'd laid out snacks and compiled a spreadsheet. For her.

Looking away, she grabbed some popcorn. What was going on with her today? The other day, she'd felt guilty for having slept leaning against Sean. Now today, she was half ready to attack him. She was all over the place.

And it wasn't the only thing her emotions were all over the place about, either. July third was seven days away. And the closer it got to the anniversary of Anthony's death, the more her emotions seemed to be riding a roller coaster. One moment, she'd feel the grief of his loss into her very bones. Then in another, she'd move from grief to feeling sorry for herself, not just for his loss, but for not having someone to share life with. Even though she didn't want that. Not anymore. And then she'd feel mad at herself for the whole mess of it.

Finally, the movie started.

Eyes on the big TV, she whispered, "How many movies are there?"

"Sshh," he whispered. She bit back a smile.

This movie wasn't funny like 'Deadpool', but she was enjoying it well enough. And then there was this scene where the main character, Steve Rogers, jumped on top of what he thought was a live grenade to protect everyone else, while they all tried to hide or run. It raised the hair on her arms, because she'd seen that kind of maybe-stupid-but-definitely-selfless courage more than once while she was deployed. And it made the movie immediately relatable to her on a visceral level.

Now, she was hooked.

It definitely did *not* hurt that once Steve received the super-soldier serum, he turned into a six-foot-tall *god* with ripped muscles and mad fighting skills.

Hmm, like someone else I know. Though Sean was taller than six feet...

Seriously not helping yourself here, Dani.

Right.

Then there was Peggy Carter, a resistance fighter and soldier who fought alongside Captain America. She was a badass. And Sean had compared Dani to this character, which now struck her as sorta flattering. Proving that Dani was all the way ridiculous.

But then came the end. "Wait. What?" Dani said, peering over at Sean. "This is sad! This isn't okay with me."

Sean nodded. "I know. Just wait until 'Infinity War'. But did you like it?"

"Yeah." She looked back to the screen as the end credits rolled. "It was really good, actually. But I'm feeling a little emotional about that ending over here."

"The next movie will make that better. I promise."

Which was how she and Sean ended up sitting on his couch all day, eating a crap-ton of popcorn, pausing only to heat up a lasagna for dinner that Sean's station chief had dropped off for him, and now found themselves starting their fourth movie.

Dani was having fun.

Like, she couldn't remember the last time she'd just hung out like this. No agenda. No rushing around. Just hanging out and relaxing with a friend.

She lived her whole life around the idea of Keep Fucking Going—but shouldn't that be about more than just clocking in and doing a job? However important that job might be? Life wasn't just about making a paycheck or even making a contribution, it was about finding joy along the way. About finding connection and meaning. All of a sudden, Dani wasn't sure she'd been doing a great job at the *living* part of life. The thoughts sat uncomfortably on her shoulders.

As 'Ironman 2' began, Dani found it hard to concentrate, and finally peered over at Sean. "So...which superhero are you? Like, I'd happily be either Peggy or Captain Marvel. Are you Captain America or Ironman?" She grabbed a handful of popcorn.

He closed his eyes. "Just give me a second. I'm picturing you in a superhero costume over here. Mmm."

She slugged him in the biceps, probably hurting her knuckles more than his stupid muscular arm. "Shut up."

Chuckling, he said, "You're the one who put the idea in my head. You can hardly blame me." On a sigh, he shook his head. "Okay, fine. Uh, if I'm anyone, it's Deadpool. Maybe Star-Lord, but probably Deadpool."

"Who's Star-Lord? And what number movie is he?" She gave him a look.

He chuckled and waved a hand. "Don't worry about it."

"Okay, then, so why Deadpool? Excels in sarcasm and irreverence?" She grinned.

He smirked. "You got me. But also, Captain America's too much of a hero and a Boy Scout for me to be him. Ironman's way too fucking smart. Bruce, who turns into the Hulk, is prolly also too smart and is super emotionally sensitive, which...not my strong suit. Spiderman's too young and pure of heart, so not me either." He shrugged. "I mean, Thor's a brooding god, so I might be able to pull that off, but otherwise I probably most identify with the soldier-turned-mercenary with the foul mouth who doesn't consider himself any kind of hero."

Dani blinked. They were just messing around, but unless she was reading into it too much, that answer revealed *all kinds of things*—less-than-generous things—about how Sean viewed himself. And she was kinda gobsmacked by it. "Sean—"

Both of their cell phones went off at the same time, hers ringing, his buzzing.

Sean paused the movie. "What the shit? Oh, it's Jesse," he said as he answered. "Yo, J."

A glance at her cell revealed Tara was calling her. "What are you two up to?" Dani said by way of answering.

"Uh, what do you mean?" Tara said.

"I'm at Sean's, who's on the phone with your hot bomb squad cop as we speak."

Sean made a face at her, one that read just a little jealous. Interesting. She arched a challenging brow at him.

Down the line, Tara chuckled. "Oh, ha. If I'd known that, we would've only called one of you. How's Sean doing?"

Looking right at the man in question, Dani said, "He's almost back to being his regular pain-in-the-ass self, so pretty good."

He blew her a kiss, then said into his phone, "Uh, sure, I'm game for that."

"I'm glad to hear it," Tara said. "So, you're hanging out, huh?"

She heard what Tara was insinuating loud and clear. "Yep. So what's up?"

"Fine, I'll ask again when you two aren't together," her

friend said, her tone full of humor. "I wanted to see if you were coming to WFC on Saturday."

Dani frowned. Didn't she usually attend? "Uh, yeah. Why?"

"No reason, really. I have news I wanted to share with everyone at dinner, so I was hoping you'd be there."

News that Jesse was calling Sean about, too, apparently. Dani's thoughts whirled on the possibilities. "Ooh, spill now."

Tara laughed. "No way. But I'm glad I'll see you soon."

"Okay, *fine,*" Dani said, smiling. "And me too."

"Have fun with Sean." There was so much innuendo in those words. Again.

"Good-bye, *Tara,*" Dani said in a sing-song tone. They hung up. "Well that was interesting." She looked at Sean. "What did Jesse say?"

"Just that they had news to share and he hoped I might come out on Saturday, at least to dinner if not WFC." He raked a hand through his short dark hair. "Tara?"

"Pretty much the same, except she said it was her news, not their news."

"Maybe they found a house," Sean said. "They've been looking."

Dani nodded. "Could be. So are you gonna go to dinner?"

Sean shrugged. "Yeah. Why not?"

"I can pick you up if you want."

"Nah, that's out of your way. Just text me where and I'll Uber. I kinda had a bigger favor to ask anyway." His lips pressed into a tight line, like he was debating saying whatever he'd been about to say. "Shit, never mind."

"What is it? I'll help if I can. I'm not just here to eat all your popcorn." Speaking of which, she grabbed herself another handful of caramel.

He chuckled. "My popcorn is your popcorn."

"Okay, now I'm wondering just how broadly this principle applies," she said, tone full of teasing.

"What d'ya mean?"

"You've said that same thing about 'Deadpool', your shower, and now your popcorn."

His eyes narrowed and he tilted his head. "Oh." He laughed and shrugged. Then he slanted her a look. "How broadly would you like it to apply, Daniela?"

Her heart tripped into a sprint. Because that look combined with that tone came across as way more than playful.

It was challenging. It was gritty. It was freaking hot.

And it sounded a helluva lot like an invitation.

CHAPTER NINE

SEAN SHOULD'VE PLAYED it off. He knew he should've. But he hadn't been able to resist pushing her, teasing her, challenging her. Because ever since she'd leaned over his body to try to nick his laptop and he'd laid his hands on her, he'd been strung tight. Not to mention, he was fucking enjoying spending time with her—her playfulness and laughter, how invested she was becoming in something he loved, the fact that he'd found yet more things they had in common.

And even though she was staring at him like she was thinking about fleeing, he still couldn't back down. "What else of mine would you like to have?"

She swallowed hard and gave a single shake of her head. "Nothing." It came out as a whisper.

He turned toward her. "You sure about that?"

Sean fully expected her to say "yes" and then they'd play it off and get back to 'Ironman 2'. But what she said was, "You're hurt."

For a split second he was confused about how that followed from what he'd asked, and then realization hit him over the head like a fucking sledgehammer. She wanted something that she worried he was too injured to give.

Or do.

Holy shit. She wanted...him.

Sore chest be damned, he was hard in a fuckin' instant.

Sean moved closer, his knee touching her thigh. "Not *that* hurt." His heart played a bass beat. "What is it you want from me, D? Name it."

She ducked her chin, her gaze going to her jeans-covered lap, where she was worrying at a silver wrap ring in the shape of two feathers that she always wore on the middle finger of her right hand. Dani took a deep breath and lifted her head to nail him with a stare. "Nothing. It's not a good idea."

"What's not a good idea?" He leaned closer.

"Whatever is...happening between us."

She felt it, too? "What's happening?" He was dying to know how she'd describe it.

"This...*pull*."

Heat lanced through his veins. "Fuck, Daniela. I feel it, too."

She licked her lips, and a beautiful flush spread over her face. "Sean, I..."

When she didn't finish her sentence, he laid it out plain. "Whatever it is you want, whatever it is you need, you can use me to have it."

"Jesus," she whispered.

"Or, tell me 'no' and I'll drop it. We'll watch 'Ironman' and eat popcorn and try to forget that this heat exists between us whether we want it to or not."

"I just want to get out of my head, but I don't want to use you to do it." The words spilled out of Dani in a rush, opening up all sorts of questions in Sean's mind. First among them was what was going on that made her need to get out of her own head? Because, fuck, he knew what that was like.

But if what she needed was a distraction, he could be that for her. "What if I want you to use me?"

Sean wasn't sure if he moved first or she did, but in the next moment, they were all over each other. Mouths fused, his hands in her long hair, her hands gripping hard on his shoulders. His tongue swept into her mouth, and she tasted salty and sweet. Perfect. With one hand, he trailed his touch down her body— over her breast, down her ribs, until he finally grasped her ass and pulled her closer.

"Fuck," she whispered. "You're hurt."

He shook his head. "I'm okay." Their kisses grew urgent, frantic, almost aggressive. She was moaning into his mouth, and the sound went right to his dick. He kissed her cheek, her neck, her ear. "What do you need from me?"

"I...I don't know." She tilted her head back, a surrender to the explorations of his mouth, and one of her hands gripped his ass.

"Want to know what I want then?" He tore at the Velcro straps around his chest, almost frantically trying to free himself from the ice machine's padding.

Swallowing hard under his lips, she nodded.

"I wanna put my mouth on you, Dani." He wanted her shattered by pleasure, and he wanted to be the one to do it. In case she regretted this later, at least she'd have that.

"Yes," she rasped, helping him unstick a bit of Velcro he couldn't reach.

Finally free, he pushed her back onto the big sofa. His gaze connected with hers, and he unbuttoned her jeans and slid those and her black panties off. Arching her back, she pulled off the dark green V-neck she'd worn, leaving her in an almost sheer lacy black bra.

For a moment, all he could do was stare at the picture she made sprawled out against the buttery black leather of his couch. Her beautiful curves, the warm tan of her skin, the neat triangle of black hair where her thighs met. Fucking gorgeous, every inch.

Sean went to his knees on the floor, his hands smoothing over her thighs, then gently pressing them open. He ran kisses up her inner thighs until his nose pressed against the soft skin between her legs. She gasped, and her hips raised.

He ran his fingers over her slit, finding her already wet. He strummed at her clit with his thumb, flicking at it with a firm pressure and a steady rhythm that made her moan. "Lick me," she said.

He arched a brow at her. "I've waited nine months for this again. Don't fuckin' rush me."

Her eyes widened and her gaze bored into him. He'd probably said more than he should've, but just then he didn't care. "But I need more."

He put his thumb in his mouth, her scent and the hint of her taste absolutely delicious, and then returned to teasing her with his now saliva-slicked touch.

"Fuck," she said. "Please, Sean."

It was the begging that did it.

He came at her like a starving man. Licking and mouthing her, alternating between teasing and tormenting her clit, and long, unhurried drags of his tongue through her folds to her opening. Her legs spread wider, allowing him to get himself good and settled there, which he fuckin' did.

While he feasted on her, he ran his hands up her body. She was lean and petite, though she was so strong that he never thought of her as small. But feeling the slight curve of her belly and the narrow span of her ribs in his hands brought home how much bigger he was. His hands splayed over her lace-covered breasts and his thumbs teased and squeezed her nipples until she was trembling beneath him.

God, her pleasure made him feel fuckin' powerful. He wanted more of it. He wanted *all* of it.

He latched his mouth around her clit, sucking and flicking his tongue over it as she thrust her hips upward, silently begging for more. A hand clutched at his shoulder, and then fingers tugged at his shirt.

"Off," she whispered, peering down at him.

Reluctantly easing his mouth off of her, Sean frowned. "I'm not pretty like you are."

"You're fucking hot, and I want to see you."

Well, when she put it like that. He tugged the tee over his head and threw it aside. And then his mouth and his hands were on her again, his thumbs gently parting her soft folds so he could devour her. Which was exactly what he did, sucking and flicking and licking until her hips were grinding against his mouth and she was holding his head down, her fingers scrabbling for purchase in his short hair.

He tried to commit the feeling of her being desperate for him to memory. Because it was the best he'd felt in a long-ass time.

A shudder ran through her whole body until she was holding her breath and pressing his head down so hard. She came on a high-pitched moan that made him feel fuckin' victorious, her hips shaking, her thighs squeezing at his shoulders, her cum making her wetter.

He didn't want this to be over. Not by a long shot. He wasn't sure what they were or weren't, but moments like this made him want to try to find out. Not that she would want that, or him, not for the long-term. And not that he had any experience being with someone for anything beyond sex.

You'd just end up hurting her anyway...

The thought was a sucker-punch of brutal reality.

So when her body settled, he lapped at her, memorizing

every little gasping moan she unleashed and wanting everything she'd given him.

In case it was all he got.

***

MORE THAN A LITTLE blown away by the force of her orgasm, Dani peered down over her belly. Seeing Sean's big body filling up the space between her thighs was stunningly sexy, especially when he glanced up at her while he licked at her over-sensitive flesh.

She couldn't stop gasping and moaning every time his tongue stroked over her clit, but it felt too damn good to make him stop. "That was freaking amazing," she said, wanting him to know. Not just by the actions of her body. She wanted to give him the words, too. Somehow, she felt like he needed them.

"I can do this all day." His breath tickled against her skin.

She knew that from experience, remembering how relentless he could be in giving oral sex. It was definitely one of his best qualities. But she'd been honest when she said she wanted to get out of her head. Even now, her brain was trying to insert itself where she didn't want it by dredging up why this wasn't a good idea, analyzing why she'd given in to this now, not to mention other things she didn't want to be thinking about. So just then, she wanted Sean to overwhelm her with everything he had.

"I know, but I'd really like to feel you inside me."

"Jesus, your mouth," he said, thunking his head against her hip.

"Problem?" She arched a brow.

He gave her a hungry look. "Hell, no. There's nothing sexier than a woman who knows what she wants and asks for it." Sean pushed to his knees, giving her a good view of just how hard he was under those jeans, and undid his button and zipper. He shoved them down over his hips, baring the thick, heavy length of his cock and those strong thighs. His denim hit the floor with a soft but satisfying *thud*.

Dani hadn't been with another man since the two of them had hooked up last October. Now that she'd finally surrendered to the chemistry and desire that'd hummed between them ever since, she was suddenly ravenous for him. She got up so she could grab her purse—

Strong arms encircled her from behind. "Where d'ya think you're going?"

Jesus, the feel of him. Tall. Muscled. His cock against her ass. She unleashed a shaky breath. "Was just getting a condom." She hoped he wasn't weirded out by her having one, but she didn't expect anyone else to be responsible for taking care of her body, so she carried some.

"Mmm." That was his only reaction, and it was a sound full of approval. So she retrieved the packet from the purse's inside zipper compartment. Meanwhile, Sean's mouth latched onto the side of her neck. Explored the sensitive hollow just below her ear. Nipped down the tendon to her shoulder. She shivered. And that was before he asked, "How do you want me?"

The question made her core squeeze. *Inside* was really the only answer that mattered to her. But she supposed she did want to see and feel all his power moving over her this time, something that hadn't happened in the dark and confined space of his truck cab where they hadn't even fully undressed. "I want you on top, pinning me down."

He spun her around, his dark eyes blazing. And Jesus he was so much taller than her. Broader and bulkier, too. "Do you just want my weight on you or are you asking me to hold you down?"

Both. That was the answer that got stuck in her throat. But she couldn't give voice to it because her brain was tripping over the fact that he'd taken the time to ask, to be clear, and to be careful with her. She pushed up onto tiptoes, bringing their lips whisper close. "Both," she finally admitted, kissing him.

As he deepened the kiss, his arms came around her, pulling her in tight against all his hardness. Her resistance to the closeness came only from her worry that she'd hurt his chest, and then he lifted her off her feet and laid her out on the leather.

She gasped. "Sean, be careful."

"I'm good, trust me. Don't you worry." He knelt between her knees, opened the packet, and rolled on the condom.

"I don't want you to hurt yourself." Second-guessing this whole thing, she said, "Maybe, I should be on top."

"Nuh-uh." He tilted his head and gave her a small smile. "Now stop thinking and take off your bra. I want access to all of you."

The words lashed heat over her, and she was quick to comply. Who thought she'd find his maddening bossiness so hot in bed?

And then he was coming down on top of her, his fingers testing her readiness until his touch glided in her slickness. Finally, he guided himself inside of her.

Dani moaned at the onslaught of sensation. His thickness penetrating her, opening her, filling her. One of his arms hooked behind a knee and spread her wider. His solid weight pressed her into the supple leather, and his other hand grasped hers and held it down above her head.

It was utter freaking perfection.

"You're so fuckin' gorgeous, Daniela," he said, looking her eye to eye as he bottomed out inside her.

His words and his actions were a full-body assault—setting her mind to spinning, her heart to tripping, and her muscles to bracing as she accepted his weight. Her back arched at the fullness, the pressure against her G-spot, the dragging friction as he pulled back out. His hips swung on a slow, grinding pace, his hip bones falling against her thighs in a way she hoped left marks. She threw her other arm above her head and whimpered at how erotic it was when he adjusted his grip to pin both of her wrists.

"You like that? Me holding you down?" In his arousal, the intensity in his expression almost read as harsh. And it was freaking hot.

"Yes," she said, meeting the scorching heat of his gaze. And damn she'd been right to want to experience him on top of her. Because those mountainous shoulders were a thing of beauty, his face was a mask of fierce masculine desire, and his weight nearly overwhelmed her in all the best ways.

His strokes drove home faster, harder, and he rolled his hips to grind his pubic bone against her clit. "Feels so fuckin' good," he said, voice gravelly and low.

She tested her hands against her grip, but he had her well secured. Pleasure zinged through her lower belly.

He arched a brow. "You okay?"

"More than. Was just testing."

"Christ, Dani. When I've got all my strength back, we're exploring whatever the hell you mean by that. You hear me?"

Her libido loved the hell out of that promise, so she nodded. Even though her brain posed the inconvenient question about whether there'd be another time, when she'd been so determined that there wouldn't be a *this* time. God, she really didn't want to think. "Harder," she pleaded.

Sean gave her what she asked for. His hips pistoned into her on a series of hard snaps that hit her just right. The sounds of skin meeting skin, her moans, and his deep, throaty groans surrounded them.

And then he adjusted his position—bracing his upper body

above her using the hand holding her wrists, and putting one foot down on the ground. His thrusts came even harder now, faster too, until she was gasping and moaning and right on the verge of coming.

"Aw, fuck, you're tight. You gonna give it to me?"

"Yes," she moaned. "So close."

His hips swiveled when he bottomed out, and it felt so good she had to close her eyes. "Want you to come all over my cock, D."

The dirty talk in that deep, almost-growl was the end of her.

Her body detonated in a bone-meltingly good orgasm that had her trembling and arching. And crying out Sean's name.

He didn't let up on her one bit, fucking her in a way that drew her release out longer and longer until she was nearly dizzy. And then he dropped down on top of her. Giving her all his weight, he hunched his body around her and hammered himself inside her hard and fast and deep. He was all she felt and saw and smelled. Suddenly, his voice filled her ears as he groaned his release, his whole body shuddering atop hers even as his hips jerked.

"Fuck, Daniela," he rasped as his movements slowed. He brought his face to hers, his eyes searching hers even as he kissed her. And it was shockingly intimate. Possibly the most intimate moment she'd shared with another person in six years. For him to be inside her, both of them raw and spent from the pleasure they'd shared, eye to eye, while he brushed her lips with kisses again and again.

He saw her. He was *with* her here. She was the farthest away from being alone as she'd been in years.

It was amazing and exciting. It was absolutely terrifying.

"You good?" he asked.

"Yeah. You?"

His grin was sexy and sincere. "I'm fuckin' terrific."

She chuckled, trying to ignore the whirl of emotion spinning in her head and tightening in her chest.

Gently, he released her leg and wrists. "Shit, I hope I didn't mark you," he said, staring at her hands.

She brought one close enough to see the dark red rings surrounding her wrist. "I wouldn't complain if you did."

One sexy eyebrow shot way up. "Don't blame me if I remember that for the next time."

The next time.

He reached between them and withdrew from her, one hand fisting around the condom. "Lemme get rid of this." Sean pushed off the couch and crossed to the bathroom. It was the first time she'd seen his body fully naked, and he was every bit as impressive as she thought he'd be. The broad shoulders. The way his ink-covered back muscles flexed. The taut roundness of his ass.

And oh, man, that ass. Dead. She was dead.

She heard the sink run, and then he was returning to her, comfortable with his nudity and feeling quite fine if that newly returned swagger meant anything. So she enjoyed the opportunity to ogle him. Because he *was* really freaking fine. "Wow."

"I know. It looks like shit, doesn't it?" His hand went to his chest. "Doesn't hurt as much now though."

How could he think that she'd meant her exclamation as anything but appreciative? And it wasn't the first time he'd been so self-deprecating. "Sean Riddick."

Her stern tone had him looking at her, his expression full of confusion. "What?"

"Sit." She pointed at the couch.

"Ooh, I like this game already." He hurried to sit.

She straddled him, one eyebrow arched. Those big hands cupped her ass, and they felt so good on her that she had to swallow hard. "This isn't a game, asshole."

said, really fuckin' glad to call her friend. Because once again, she was going above and beyond for him today.

"Aha," the doc said. "Daniela, welcome. Don't hesitate to chime in if you have any questions." She nodded.

They reviewed his history and the doc asked him whether he'd been having any trouble with pain, dizziness, headaches, or nausea, all of which were negatives with the exception of those first few days. And then it was moment-of-truth time.

"Let's take off this shield and see how you're healing."

Sean's stomach tossed as the man carefully pealed the tape away from his forehead and cheekbone, leaving a pad of gauze underneath.

"I'm going to dim the lights now." Dr. Herschel pressed a button on the panel of controls and then removed the gauze. "Tell me how things look to you before I do my examination."

Blowing out a breath, Sean opened his injured eye. His heart was a freight train in his chest as he waited for his brain to register the world around him. "It's clearer." He looked at Dani, whose expression was so hopeful for him. He wasn't sure how he lucked into having her on his side these days, but he really fuckin' appreciated it. "It's clearer than it was last week." He forced himself to focus. On Dani's pretty face. The clock. The eye chart being projected on the far wall. He couldn't read all the lines like he normally could, except for those teeny tiny ones at the bottom that prolly no fuckers could. "I'm not sure it's back to normal though."

"Let me take a closer look." For the next ten minutes, the doctor conducted his examination.

The first time Doc shined a light directly into Sean's eye, he cringed. "Aah, stings."

"Photosensitivity is not surprising and should not be a lasting problem once you're no longer wearing the eye covering."

His eyes went wide. "Wait, how did we go from orgasm to asshole in under two minutes?"

His way with words nearly made her smile. Gently, she laid one hand against his chest. "This isn't ugly to me. It's an injury. One that means you survived when that fucking truck hit you and scared the shit out of me. I was expressing admiration for your body, not criticizing your appearance. I would never do that, even if you hadn't just been inside me two minutes ago."

"Oh."

"Uh huh."

His gaze dropped somewhere between them, fanning his long dark lashes against his cheek. "You were scared for me?"

Dani huffed. And then she grasped his face in both of her hands. She wasn't sure what was happening between them. Or what they were to one another. But she knew this. "I'm not better than you. I hated that you said that, and I hated that I made you feel that way. And of-fucking-course I was scared for you. You're my friend, and you're a good man. Someone who risks himself to help other people. I know I give you a hard time sometimes—"

"Sometimes?" He smirked at her, though he didn't quite pull it off, and it was obvious to her that he was trying to inject humor to deflect from the seriousness of what she was saying. Jesus, he *was* freaking Deadpool.

But just then, she wasn't having it. "I'm being serious."

"I know. You're not the one that made me feel that way, D. Okay? It wasn't you." There was a vulnerability in those dark eyes that nearly stole her breath and emphasized the gravity of the admission he'd just made. *Someone* had told him or taught him that he was less than, and it was a lesson that seemed to have stuck. Something in the center of Dani's chest squeezed.

Sean blinked and glanced away, and suddenly he looked just like she'd felt a few moments before—*too seen.*

That was some good news, at least. Since, you know, fires were fuckin' bright. He breathed a sigh of relief. "So, what's it looking like, Doc?"

"Just one moment." The man pushed the equipment away, typed at the keyboard for what seemed like forfuckin'ever, and then turned back to Sean. "The affected eye is at 20/70 right now, whereas your other eye is 20/20. It's only been six days since the injury, and there's some corneal inflammation that's likely contributing to the differential—and probably accounts for your photosensitivity, too. The cornea helps focus the light that comes into the eye and is responsible for a large part of the eye's focusing power. So my best guess is that we'll continue to see improvement in the vision as the inflammation heals, and I recommend that we continue to shield the eye to avoid strain and let that cornea rest and heal."

Sean swallowed hard. After Dani left last night, he'd made his way upstairs to his bed for the first time all week, but then he'd laid there awake for a long time. His head full of churn and burn over a million and one things. First, what being with Dani again meant, if anything. Second, what he wanted it to mean. And, hell, he didn't know since he'd never expected to happen it again in the first place. Plus there were some mentions of *a next time* floating around out there that he was totally game for, but that led him back to topic number one all over again. Third, he replayed that moment afterward when she'd called him on his BS, along with the unusual admission he'd made to her—one that surprised even himself. His shitty childhood wasn't something he often discussed, and yet he'd referenced it twice with Dani.

And, of course, his brain hadn't been able to stop worrying about this appointment. Which was why, at about two o'clock in the morning, he found himself for probably the dozenth fucking time re-reading the NFPA's standards for firefighters' professional qualifications, which DCFD followed.

There were several things that concerned him. Any residuals of contusions or lacerations which impaired the visual function required for satisfactory performance of fire duty were disqualifying. And freaking corneal inflammation likely fell under that. And the standards for visual acuity were fucking confusing, but seemed to require uncorrected vision better than 20/40 in one eye and 20/100 in the other. Unless he'd read it wrong. Which, who the fuck knew.

He blinked at the man sitting in front of him. *That guy* would know. "Doc, maybe you can explain something to me." He pulled out his cell and went to his photos. Because he'd screenshot the shit out of the quals. "I'm a firefighter. And I need to be able to meet certain visual standards. What does this mean?" He held out his phone.

The doctor adjusted his glasses as he looked at the screen. "It means you meet the standards for visual acuity, Mr. Riddick." Sean could've fallen off the chair in relief. He glanced at Dani, who was smiling at him like he'd won the lottery. Dr. Herschel continued, "Your vision without correction is stronger than these minimum requirements. And if the injured eye doesn't improve to 20/20, we can always consider soft contact lenses for the one eye, depending on your comfort. Either way, this is not a concern."

"So am I out of the woods, then? After this finishes healing?"

"As long as there's no lasting damage to the cornea that impairs your function, the prognosis is hopeful."

Fuck. Why did that feel less hopeful than he'd, well, hoped for. "Uh, okay."

"Dr. Herschel," Dani said, "Is there any reason to be

concerned about infection? Would there be any value in a preventative course of antibacterial drops?"

"I'm not seeing any signs of infection, and the most acute time for such a concern would've been in the immediate aftermath of the accident. As you know, noninfectious keratitis usually heals on its own, and nothing I'm seeing leads me to believe Mr. Riddick suffers from it."

Dani nodded. "It's good news, Sean."

He gave her a hard look. "Really?

She smiled, and there was nothing but sincerity on her face. "You're getting better."

He nodded but couldn't quite wipe the frown off his face, because what if better wasn't good enough? What would he even be without firefighting?

Outside on the street, the day was breezy and hot, the sun bright in the late June sky. From a block away, the dome of the Capitol building towered over this part of the city, gleaming white in the sunshine.

"Hey," Dani said, a hand on his arm.

He peered down at her, suddenly aware he was being a sullen asshole. "Sorry."

She shook her head. "Anyone would be worried in your shoes. But what I heard in there was positive. I promise."

"Okay." God, he wanted to kiss her, but he wasn't sure where they stood. She'd left his house around ten last night, and they'd kissed at her car when he'd walked her outside. But he wasn't any fuckin' good at reading this kind of thing. "Can I buy you lunch as a thank you?"

She glanced at her cell and twisted her lips. "Sorry. I have to be back by one. I'll see you at dinner tomorrow night, though?"

"Yeah, o'course. And no apologies. Can I call you an Uber at least? You know, since you came over here for me and all."

The smile she gave him was a little amused and a lot sexy

and did absolutely nothing good for his desire to kiss her. Right here on the street. Where everyone would know she was his. And he was hers. But since he didn't think any of that was actually true—hot sex aside—he stood right where he was.

"I'm just gonna take the Metro. It's easy."

He nodded. "Yeah. Sure. I'll see you tomorrow then. Have a good day."

"Thanks." She glanced up at him for a long moment. Belatedly, it occurred to him that she seemed to be hesitating and uncertain, too. But before he figured out whether that meant anything, she took a step backwards. Another. And then she was walking away.

Fuck. Why did he feel like he'd just messed something up?

He sighed. And tried to decide what the hell to do with himself.

"Hey, Riddick?"

His gaze cut down the sidewalk to where Dani was waiting to cross the intersection. "I bet it feels *huge* in this hand." She raised a hand and waved.

He barked out a laugh. Fuckin' quoting 'Deadpool' to him. As if Daniela England hadn't already been hot before. She seemed to get more appealing with every new thing he learned, making him wonder why and how it was that they'd known each other all these years and never really managed to go beyond their respective sarcastic surfaces to learn anything much at all.

Sean didn't know the answer to that, so he waved back, something uncomfortable swelling in his chest. Dani disappeared amid the throngs of tourists and government workers on their lunch breaks.

An idea coming to mind, Sean called himself an Uber. Maybe spending some time at the station would make him feel more grounded.

Twenty minutes later, Sean found himself in Columbia

Heights standing in front of a long, two-story tan building with three bright red bay doors and matching trim on the windows—the home of Company 11.

The best truck company in the city. No, the world. No matter what the boys in the city's other companies said.

The center bay door stood open, so Sean walked inside the garage, past the big, long ladder truck and around the new Seagrave pumper. Off to the left, everyone's personal protective equipment hung on racks—some of it brown with yellow reflective stripes, which he still wore, and some of it the city's new black and yellow—ready and waiting for the next call.

The company's emblem was emblazoned on a large cut-out sign hanging on the wall above the gear—a skull and cross bones, of a sort. It had a grinning skull wearing a black fire helmet labeled with the 4th battalion insignia, with a length of hose and a Halligan bar crossed behind. Above the helmet were the words, *House of Flame.*

He didn't find anyone in the garage, which meant the guys were probably either upstairs in the dorms, hanging out in the day-room, or chowing in the mess hall. But since one of the rear bay doors was open, too, he poked his head outside. The space behind the fire house consisted of a large diagonal parking lot for their personal vehicles. It was also where they washed their trucks.

And it was where they grilled when the weather was good and the guys on mess duty had barbecuing skills. Sean smelled the mouthwatering aroma of grilled meat before he found three of his brothers shooting the shit around the big Coleman.

"How many firefighters does it take to grill some burgers and dogs?" he called out.

They turned to see him standing there, everybody grinning and exclaiming his name.

"Yo, Sean, good to see you," Tucker Jacobs said with a bit of a southern accent as he waved the grill tongs. He was one of the best cooks of the group, and everyone was always happy when Tuck was in charge of their chow.

"You, too. Looks like I came at the right time." Sean waggled his brows at the grill.

Tuck winked. "I've got more than enough meat here for everyone."

Sean smirked. "That's not what the ladies say."

Everyone chuckled even as Tucker glared. "Just for that, you get the one that fell on the ground, Riddick."

"Hey, man," Jeff Evans said, coming to shake Sean's hand. Jeff was one of the old timers in the house, old enough that he remembered when their station house was brand new back in '84. But he could stretch the line as good as or even better than a lot of the younger men. And he was a hilarious storyteller to boot. "See what happens to you when you're not on a job?"

Nodding, Sean shrugged. "You shoulda seen the other guy, though."

Jeff pointed at him. "I believe it."

Next to greet him was one of their probies, Seth Malone, a twenty-two-year-old who Sean liked to hassle for preferring DC Comics over Marvel. They clasped hands. "How you doing, Sean? It's good to see you."

"You, too. What's been going on?" Sean asked the group, a part of him feeling more at ease for being here.

"We stretched three times last night," Tuck said, adjusting the DCFD baseball cap on his head. "Structure fires all three times. It was fucking crazy."

"I heard the sirens at least twice," Sean said. It was part of what had kept him awake and on edge last night—not being here to help. "You the black cloud around here, probie?" He teased Seth for cursing them with the high frequency of calls. Some people loved a "black cloud" because they wanted to be out there fighting the fire as much as possible, whereas other people prized the "white clouds" whose presence seemed to chase all the calls away. For himself, Sean probably fell on the side of keeping busy. Black clouds were okay by him.

Seth groaned. "Not you, too. It ain't my fucking fault." Everyone laughed, razzing him mercilessly because he let them see that it got under his skin. Rookie mistake.

"Chief said you're off for a whole month," Jeff said. "That true?"

"Fuckin' A, probably. I gotta wait for my eye to heal and I've got a chest wall injury that makes shit difficult." Not that he'd ever admit it to Dani, but his chest was a lot sorer today than it'd been yesterday before they christened his black leather couch. He'd actually given in to some pain meds last night, too. Worth it, though. So damn worth it.

"So how stir crazy are you going?" Tuck peered over at him as he flipped the burgers.

Sean crossed his arms, then uncrossed them again when his body immediately began to protest the movement. "This week wasn't too bad, but yeah, I can feel it coming."

Meow. The sound was accompanied by a soft rubbing against Sean's calf.

"Hey, Winston. Did you miss me?" Sean leaned down and scooped the old boy into his arms. He was grey-striped with patches of all-white fur here and there. He meowed again and curled his head into Sean's palm as he petted him. "I think you did."

Tucker filled a tray with dogs and another with burgers. "All right, probie. Grab a platter and lunch is served."

Seth moved his ass like a probie should and then all four of them—well, four a half with Winston—went upstairs to the mess hall. The station's living quarters weren't fancy—the floors were a cream-colored linoleum, the walls a plain off-white, the

furniture in the dorm rooms generally spartan. But the camaraderie more than made up for the lack of decor in the day-room
and the plastic chairs in the mess hall.

By the time they made it up the steps, Winston was purring
like a little engine in his hands. Sean swung into the mess hall
with the others, and it only took about five seconds for one of the
ten or so guys gathered there to do a double-take at his presence.
Greetings echoed around the room, causing Winston to swan
dive out of his arms.

"Riddick!" a guy about his age named Jersey called out.

"Welcome back, man!" Bobby clapped him on the back.
And then the guy cringed. "Shit, sorry."

"You're good, B, no worries," Sean said, shaking another
guy's hand. And another.

Chief came around the table and held out a hand. "How are
ya, kid?"

They shook, and Sean met the older man's gaze. "Getting
better every day."

"That's what I like to hear. But I thought you were
supposed to be, you know, relaxing." The man shook his head.

"I can sit on my ass here with you fine people as easily I can
sit on my ass at home." Everyone chuckled.

"But you can only eat my meat here, Riddick," Tucker said
to a round of raucous replies and loud guffaws.

Sean held his hands up. "I literally don't know what to say
to that."

He settled in at one of the tables and piled a plate high. He
answered everyone's questions about what happened to him.
When conversation turned to all the routine things firefighters
complained or talked about, Sean reveled in the normalcy of it.
Damn, being here was good for his mood. Maybe he should've
come around sooner, even if he wasn't in fighting condition
right now.

He'd eaten about half his burger when the two-tone alert went off in a series of high-low tones that meant one thing: structure fire. The lights in the mess hall blinked and the digital screen above the door lit up, the text matching the dispatcher's mechanical voice. "Engine eleven. Truck six. Structure fire. 1428 Meridian Place, Northwest. Time out: two minutes fifteen seconds."

That was damn close.

People were off their asses as soon as the tones went off. Guys called hasty good-byes to Sean as they choked down the last of their burgers and dogs. Except for him and a pair of EMTs whose rig hadn't been called, the room had cleared out in about thirty seconds.

Well, fuck.

Downstairs the trucks started up, their engines rumbling on an echo in the garage. And then the rumble deepened as they pulled out onto 14th Street, their sirens wailing to part the inevitable traffic in front of the fire house.

"I guess we're on clean-up," one of the EMTs said to the other.

"I'll help," Sean said, because if he didn't have something to do with his hands right goddamn now, he was going to lose his shit. It'd been good to come see the guys. It made him feel like he was a part of something again. It'd grounded him and reminded him of who he was—or who he was trying to be. And it'd gotten him out of his own feels about what was or wasn't happening with Dani.

But watching his buddies leave while he sat there twiddling his fuckin' thumbs?

No. That was unsat in the extreme. He should be out there watching their backs. Instead, he was limited to being a damn scanner jockey—a non-responder whose curiosity made him need to know what was going on. If any of them got hurt, it would be in his place, or because he hadn't given them another set of hands to fight the beast.

Fuck.

When Sean finished clearing the tables, the EMTs told him they'd load the dishwasher, so he cleared out. The fire was close enough that he could smell it, and it lit a spark in his belly that made him almost restless with the need to fight.

Sean walked the two blocks down 14th to the cross street where the incident was unfolding and could just make out his guys on the heavily smoking roof of one of the row houses. He glanced at the looky-loos gathering to watch the fire and couldn't stand being one of them.

So he hoofed it back towards his house. It was less than a fifteen-minute walk, which meant no way would it be enough to release the pressure suddenly building up inside his head.

Planting his ass on the couch in his basement, he honestly didn't know what would be capable of doing that for him right now. And maybe sitting on *this* couch wasn't the best idea when he was already so wound up since it made him think of Dani and the fuckin' fantastic time he'd spent with her on it. The physical side of their relationship—or whatever it was they had —was damn near perfect. But the not really knowing what the two of them were or what they were doing added to his restless-ness and agitation...because maybe he wanted it to be some-thing. Which, fuck. Sean didn't know what to do with that kind of desire since he'd never had it before and because Daniela England was too fuckin' good for him by far.

"I'm not better than you. I hated that you said that, and I hated that I made you feel that way..."

He'd appreciated her saying that. Really, he had. But if he had any good qualities it was being able to be real and face facts. And he had a lifetime of facts that told him who he was. Sean scrubbed his hands over his face and debated what the hell to do with himself.

And then his phone *dinged* an incoming email message that answered that question—and that, surprisingly, helped calm down a little of the bullshit churning in his head.

CHAPTER ELEVEN

THE THIRD OF July was just five days away—six if you counted the rest of today. But since it was almost six o'clock, doing so made no real sense.

Bracing her gloved hands on her knees, Dani exhaled heavily and watched as her sweat dripped down on the mats. Between a busy shift and now training at WFC, she was kinda exhausted out of her mind.

That's not why your head's a mess and you know it.

Okay, fine. It was those five days being all that separated her from the anniversary. She wasn't sure why, but it seemed to be weighing on her more than usual this year, as if it was something to be dreaded or like her body and mind's restlessness were some sort of a premonition.

She looked across the circle they'd all formed around the tag-team grappling drill they were currently running and found Mo frowning at her, a question on his face. She could almost hear his deep voice asking, "You okay, D?" She gave him a nod and a small smile and forced herself to get her head back into the game. Literally.

Jesse and Jud were in the ring, both of them trying to dominate the other. This drill focused entirely on groundwork, forcing each of them to use their wrestling and grappling skills to achieve submission. A fighter's turn ended only if they had to tap out or if they got close enough to the edge to tag in a teammate.

Jesse and Jud were total opposites—Jesse was more reserved where Jud was always chatting someone up. Jesse possessed the kind of cool and calculating demeanor you'd expect from a guy who defused bombs for a living, while Jud had an infectious, playful, and gregarious personality. And Jesse had dark hair and eyes, where Jud was more fair with sandy blond hair and striking dark blue eyes. But they were pretty evenly matched in the ring, which was why they'd been at it for almost five minutes and neither had been able to achieve a submission. And right now, they were *both* shit-talking up a storm.

"Come on, old man, you gonna make a move?" Jesse taunted.

"You're only two fucking years younger than me, asshole," Jud said in a southern accent that made Dani picture the cowboy hat he sometimes wore. "Plus, I'm a lot fucking prettier." Laughter, cheers, and jeers filled the room. Jesse didn't still work on Jud's and Tara's commercial diving team, but the men's friendship obviously remained strong despite Jesse's jump over to the DCPD.

"Come on Jesse," Tara cheered, laughing when Jud threw her an exaggerated wounded look at her lack of support. Everyone laughed.

Everyone except Jesse, who used Jud's distractedness to get a hold around his chest. They struggled for a long moment, and then Jesse flipped him over and went for a rear-naked choke. He couldn't quite get it though, and they ended up in a series of attacks that brought them closer to where Dani stood just outside the circle. Jesse reached out a hand—tagging Dani in.

"Go get him, Dani," Jesse said, clapping her on the shoulder.

"Well, hi there, pretty lady," Jud said, his tone well aware that his words would irritate her. Their love of teasing, innuendo, and sarcasm was probably one of the reasons that Sean and Jud had become good friends over the past few months.

"Are you here to talk or fight?" she shot back as she got into position.

Around them, the cheering, clapping, and shit-talking escalated as Jud and Dani attacked, resisted, and fought. He'd been in the ring for a good ten minutes now, so his sweat made getting a good hold hard. In a burst of effort, Jud pushed Dani flat on her stomach. He reached for one of her legs and went to straddle her, which told Dani that he was either going for an ankle lock or a stepover toehold facelock, neither of which she was letting him get. So she rolled into a ball and then, using the last of her energy, exploded open with her knees and elbows in a way that threw him off balance.

The room erupted.

Coach blew the whistle.

Jud held out his hands as he pushed to his knees. "Aw, come on Coach Mack, I gotta redeem myself here."

Everyone laughed, including Coach. "Live to fight another day, Jud. But that was some damn good fighting." Coach pointed at her. "Dani, you're looking strong."

She nodded but felt like such a fraud. And she was still feeling that way thirty minutes later when she and Tara hit the women's locker room to get ready for dinner.

"What's up with you tonight?" Tara asked, peering at her warily, as if Dani were a cornered animal that might lash out.

Dani supposed it wasn't an unreasonable analogy since the question put her hackles up—not because Tara was out of line, but because Dani just didn't want to deal. But clearly she needed to, so she forced her shoulders to relax as she tossed her gym bag on a bench. "Just a rough week."

"Aw, I'm sorry. What's been going on? Work?" Her friend's expression was so earnest in wanting to be there for her that Dani dropped into a sitting position.

"No, things are good there. I mean, I had to tell my Department Director I wasn't taking his promotion again, but I think it might've actually penetrated his skull this time."

Tara sat beside her and tugged off her fingerless gloves. "That's good at least. So if it's not work, is it Sean? I mean, is he doing okay?"

Dani blew out a long breath, tired of keeping so much bottled up, but afraid to voice half of what was going on inside her. She'd been carrying all of her own emotional water for so long, she no longer knew how to set down the buckets. "I went to the eye doc with him yesterday and the prognosis is hopeful. I know he's still worried, but all things considered, he's really good."

Tara nodded, then smirked. "How good is he?"

Dani's brain tripped on the innuendo, on deciding whether to play it off or dismiss it entirely, and instead she freaking blushed. Brilliantly. Heat flooded her face.

"Oh, my God!" Tara's eyes went wide as she grinned. "Dani! Shut. Up. Right. Now."

She was so busted that she dropped her face into her hands and groaned.

"Oh, my God, *omigod!*" Tara pulled at one of Dani's hands until she uncovered her face. Dani peered at Tara and found her friend's expression filled with pure delight. "I need details. Big, muscular, juicy details."

Dani chuckled despite herself.

And then she sighed, debated, and let her admission fly. "So...on Thursday night, we had sex. He proved himself an orgasm-giving god among men. And now...I don't know what we are or what I want or if I even want anything." Tara's eyes got wider with every word Dani uttered. "And if you ever tell him I said he was an orgasm-giving god I will have to kill you even though I really like you."

"I won't. I promise," she whispered, even though they were the only ones in the locker room. "Wow. Wow!" Tara stared at Dani like she'd just won the lottery. If only her feelings about Sean were that clear. Or, like, even a little clear.

But now that Dani was sharing, she figured she might as well come all the way clean. "And this wasn't the first time it happened."

Tara's jaw dropped open and she slapped her gloves against the bench. "What? When?" And then her eyes narrowed into all-knowing slits. "The freaking Halloween party. Tell me I'm not right!"

"You're right."

"I knew it! I totally knew it! That's why you two have been throwing off the fuck-me-or-fight-me vibes all this time." Tara was pretty much wearing a perma-grin now.

Geez, had it really that obvious? Dani chucked her gloves into her bag and yanked out her towel. "I guess. The thing is, it's been different spending time with him this past week."

"How so?"

Sighing, Dani really thought about what she meant. "There's just a lot more to him than I realized."

And that was a problem, because Dani liked a lot of what she'd learned about the man—his playfulness, his passions, the little quirky things they had in common, like loving tomato soup and grilled cheese, or thinking cheddar and caramel popcorn tasted great together. And they had more important things in common than she'd ever known, too. In addition to being prior military, working in fields that both focused on helping people in moments of crisis, belonging to WFC, and sharing a lot of friends, Dani had been surprised to learn that her sense of humor was so similar to his. And she'd been amazed to find that she enjoyed superhero stories as much as he did, a new interest that was heightened by remembering Sean talking about how those stories had helped him through his childhood. The way he talked, he didn't have much family, and neither did she. And he liked to read, which she did, too. They even enjoyed some of the same books.

It seemed like with every new thing she learned about the man, she found something else that appealed to her. But she just didn't know if she wanted *anyone* appealing to her, damnit. Being alone got lonely, sure, but being together raised the specter of getting left behind again. Of having the person she cared about getting unexpectedly ripped away. And she just wasn't sure how much more of that she could take.

"If that's true, then why not see where it goes? What are the cons?"

Dani turned and faced her friend. On an exhale that left her feeling ancient, she let the words fly. "July third is the anniversary of my husband's death. You'd think since it's been six years, it wouldn't screw me up so much anymore, but honestly, it does. And it is." She managed a small smile when Tara grasped her hand. "So I don't know if I want to be in a relationship, with anyone. And it's really freaking hard to figure out what I feel right now when my emotions are so all over the place."

"Aw, Dani, I'm sorry. I would have to think it's totally normal for an anniversary to hit you hard like that. I mean, it's not at all the same thing, but the anniversary of my accident always makes me unsettled. Even though I see this everyday—" She fingered the long, marked scar that curved around one whole side of her neck. "—I feel the weight of it even more right before the anniversary. It's almost like a feeling of dread. As if, just because something bad happened on that date before, it's going to happen again. It's terrible and frustrating, because just when I think I'm really over it, here comes a reminder to set off my anxiety all over again."

"That's...exactly how it feels," Dani said. Unshed tears stung the backs of her eyes at finding someone who understood her so well.

"Well, look, you've known Sean a lot longer than I have, but the guy is one of the most laid-back people I know. So maybe you guys just keep it casual until you feel like you're in a better place."

Casual. Right. What were they if not casual? They'd made no promises. They had no expectations of one another. They were the same frenemies they'd always been. Something about that conclusion niggled inside Dani, but she just nodded and embraced the fact that she felt better for having let a little of these emotions out. "Thank you. Really."

Tara hugged her, and Dani let herself be pulled into it. "Also, I hear that hot sex with orgasm-giving gods is really good for stress relief."

Dani smiled. "Did Jesse tell you that?"

Tara burst out laughing. "I'm sure he has, but he also isn't wrong. Orgasm-giving gods are something we have in common, that's all I'm saying..."

Unsure how to reply to Tara's assertion, Dani just smirked and shook her head.

"Come on, let's get cleaned up," Tara said, grabbing her things for the shower. "Food will help, too. And if you need to talk or want company or need a pint of Ben & Jerry's, you know you can call me at any hour, day or night. Okay? I'll be there."

"Okay," Dani said, following Tara to the stalls at the back of the locker room. "For the record, I like chocolate chip cookie dough and mint chocolate chip. Pretty much anything with chocolate chips."

"Duly noted," Tara said, grinning at her.

In the shower, Dani leaned her head back into the hot water and let it stream down her hair and over her body. She imagined letting the stress and worry and fear wash away, a visualization technique she'd learned years ago in grief counseling. For all the good it had done her. What Dani wouldn't have given for her granny to be here now so Dani could talk and cry it out before Granny kicked her butt into shape with some no-nonsense wisdom.

Both of her grandmothers had been wonderful women in their own ways, but Nana, her father's mother, had been gutted by the loss of Dani's dad and couldn't talk about him without getting upset, so Dani stopped bringing him up to her; whereas Granny always confronted things head on and would let Dani talk about her mom and dad as much as she needed—all while making sure Dani didn't wallow in her grief for them. Dani supposed Tara had just done something like that for her, and it made her appreciate their deepening friendship even more.

By the time she was getting dressed and joining up with the rest of the WFC gang, Dani felt more like her usual self. "Hey, where are we going? I have to text Sean."

Exclamations went up around the group—everyone glad to hear he was joining them. Dani smiled at that and hoped he knew how much he was being missed around here.

Including by her. She could admit that much.

Finally, the group decided on a restaurant, a fantastic Mexican place just a few blocks away and, as they left the gym, she shot off the information to Sean.

His response came almost immediately, like he'd been waiting for her to text.

Did someone say chimichangas?

Completely confused, Dani pecked out, *Uh, I'm sure you can order them?*

And then it dawned on her. He was quoting 'Deadpool'. Because of course he was. But before she could write another reply, he sent a gif of Deadpool gasping in surprise.

Dani chuckled and sent a new reply: *I figured it out. Now, get your ass to the Cantina, Mr. Pool*

Next, Sean sent an image. Of Deadpool, facing away but peering over his shoulder coquettishly, a finger to his mouth, his hand on his ass. The caption read:

BAD ASS.
SMART ASS.
GREAT ASS.

Laughing out loud at that, Dani found a 'Deadpool' gif of her own. A close up of Deadpool's face with the caption: *Oh, I'm touching myself tonight.*

After she hit *Send*, she put her phone away. And found it hard not to grin the whole way to dinner.

CHAPTER TWELVE

By the time Sean arrived at the restaurant, everyone was already seated around a big table of nine with overflowing baskets of chips. The only open seat was on the far side right next to Dani, who was looking hot as usual tonight in a simple fitted dark gray T-shirt, her black hair laying all together over one shoulder and exposing a black ribbon choker she wore around her neck. She was mid-conversation with Tara when she saw him. Even as she finished her sentence, she smiled at him and he just knew—that empty seat by her wasn't a coincidence.

She'd saved it for him.

Now whether she did so to be near him or, you know, so she could possibly stab him with her fork was anybody's call.

Still, as everyone said hello and rose to shake his hand or hug him, anticipation and satisfaction flowed through Sean's veins.

"Hey, B, you made it," Sean said to Billy.

Billy rose and clasped his hand. "Yeah. Hey, man. Good to see you. Damn, you're looking so much better."

"Why does that sound like a backhanded compliment?"

Sean quipped, accepting Shayna's hug when she opened her arms to him. "Hey, Shay."

Her smile was pure affection and, man, did he eat it up. "Hey, big guy."

Chuckling, Billy shook his head. "No, no, you know, it's just that the last time I saw you a plate kicked your ass and now you totally look like you could take that plate *down*."

"Damn plates," Sean groused, smiling despite himself. Defeated first by a tomato soup can and then by a plate. He was not living his best life right now, that was for damn sure. "How was the game with Dante?" he asked, shifting the attention away from himself. Though that wasn't the only reason he asked. He was genuinely curious. He wasn't telling anyone yet, but one of the ways he'd dealt with his restlessness this week was by putting in an application to be a Big Brother— and yesterday afternoon he'd received an email inviting him to schedule a series of interviews. Unexpectedly, they'd had availability last night to do the first—a screening session by phone. There was nothing that got you out of your own head like helping other people—which he knew firsthand and was one of the reasons why he took on all those overtime shifts. By the time he'd finished that call and scheduled the second interview, he'd been genuinely surprised by how much better he felt. Not fantastic, but also not hanging on by a thread, either.

"We had a great time," Billy said, grinning. "I'd forgotten how much a boy can eat at the age of twelve." He put his hand on his stomach. "My thirty-three-year-old gut doesn't love that I tried to keep up. It was cool though. It was the first time Dante had ever been to a professional sporting event. He was so psyched."

"That's awesome, man," Sean said, trying to resist the hope rising inside himself that he'd get his own Little. He could already tell he was going to be disappointed if they didn't approve him. Why the shit had he done this again?

Man up, Riddick. Fine.

It took Sean about five minutes to make it the rest of the way around the table, but he wasn't complaining about any of it because he had to admit that he appreciated the pick-me-up of his friends' enthusiasm.

"Miss me?" Sean said to Dani as he finally settled into his seat.

One brow arched, she whacked his arm as she passed him a menu. "Mildly," she said with a disinterested sigh.

He grinned and leaned in close, close enough that his lips were at her ear. And damn she smelled good—like something warm and floral that made his mouth water. "Sure it wasn't more than that, D? 'Cuz I think it was more than that." He didn't think he imagined the slight shiver that ran down her neck, and that also left him feeling pretty fucking satisfied as he sat back in his chair and flipped open his menu.

"You're irritating," she said as she sipped at a margarita.

Sean chuckled. Once, her little barbs would've had him biting back irritation. But since Dani had spent the day sending him ridiculous 'Deadpool'-inspired texts, he knew this was just part of the game. And maybe it was more than that, too. Because her texts had been a big part of what allowed him to drag himself out of the suck after the day before had kicked his ass and left his body restless and his sleep fitful. The ass-kicking hadn't been physical, of course. In fact, his chest was feeling better even though it still looked like hell, and the ache from the cut near his eye had dulled into nothing more than a nagging annoyance. No, the ass-kicking had been all inside his mind where he had no fucking defense.

The waiter arrived and began taking orders, temporarily halting conversations all around the table. Sean got busy figuring out what he wanted to put in his pie hole. But the words printed on the laminated page sorta faded away as his mind drifted.

It'd surprised Sean how much missing out on working that fire with the rest of the guys had left him feeling like shit, like he was letting them down. From there, it apparently hadn't been a big jump for his brain to make to *the nightmare*.

The first time he'd jolted awake, he hadn't known why. Sitting upright in bed, all he knew was the terror surging through him. Warily, he'd fallen back to sleep, and then came the one he'd had many times before—the one based on the real-life horror he'd caused.

It started the way it always did—with an explosion.

Out of nowhere, a chip sailed over his menu and hit him in the face.

"What the shit?" he said, flinching. Jud's laughter marked him as the culprit. Sean flipped him off even as his ears tuned back into his surroundings, making him realize that someone had been saying his name. A frowning Dani tapped his arm, which was when he saw the waiter standing behind him ready to take his order. "Oh, hell, sorry. The steak fajitas and a Coke, please."

"What happened to the chimichangas?" Dani asked when he was done ordering.

Shoving away the thoughts that had gotten him all tangled inside his head—*again*, damnit all to hell—he found himself seriously appreciating the topic change, especially when Dani's frown made it clear she knew something was up. "It rocks that you understand my 'Deadpool' references now." Those references, her texts all day, her saving a seat for him—as if Dani hadn't already appealed to him...

She shrugged. "I suppose it is mildly amusing."

Sean did a double take and then gave her a cut-the-bullshit

look. "You take that back right now, woman. You might feel mildly towards me, but I heard you laughing. Maybe you forget that I was there. Ain't no fucking way you feel mildly about 'Deadpool' so go sell that bridge somewhere else."

The side of her mouth quirked. Just a little. And Sean knew he had her.

"You seem very serious about your appreciation for 'Deadpool'," Tara said from across the table.

He arched a single eyebrow. "Have you seen it?" When she shook her head, that began a rowdy conversation that lasted through much of the meal and covered everything from movies to comics to books. But *not* fighting, *not* work, *not* Sean's fuckin' injuries. Thank you very much.

That was until Mo said, "So, I've got an announcement to make." When the table quieted down and the big guy had everyone's attention, he continued. "Billy and I are going into business together."

Sitting across the table from each other, the two men were both grinning as Mo spilled the beans that Sean had been privy to a few days earlier.

"We're calling it the Griffin Security Consulting Group. Personal security, security consulting, private investigation, that sorta thing. With a priority on hiring vets."

Exclamations rose up all around. "No shit," Noah said, smiling and clapping Billy on the back. He reached across the table and shook hands with Mo. "Congratulations."

"Wow," Dani said, sitting between Sean and Mo. She twisted in her seat to give Mo a hug. "I'm so happy for you. I know you've been wanting to find a new mission and now you have."

"Amen to that," Mo said in his deep voice.

Sean raised his glass. "To Mo and Billy kicking ass and taking names!"

"Here, here!" everyone said, following suit.

Raucous conversation followed until, finally, Jesse rose and said, "Hey everyone, I have an announcement, too." When the table quieted down, he smiled down at Tara. "Actually, *we* have an announcement."

The look Tara gave Jesse nearly sucker punched Sean, because in his entire sorry life, no one had ever looked at him with that kind of utter soul-deep, unconditional love. And had Sean ever seen more peace and contentment on that guy's face? He'd only known Jesse for about six months, but he didn't think so.

Jesse urged Tara to stand up next to him. "I asked Tara to marry me, and she said yes."

Tara held up her hand and showed off her ring. "We're getting married!"

"Holy shit!" Jud said, standing up next to Jesse to shake his hand. They exchanged a one-armed hug. "Huge fucking congrats." Next, Jud went around to sweep Tara into his arms. "Happy for you, Tara."

When Dani rose beside him, Sean blinked out of his thoughts. He followed her and joined just about everyone else who'd gotten up to shake hands and give hugs. Waiting to get up closer to Jesse and Tara, Sean noticed for the first time that Dani was wearing a short black denim skirt and a pair of black Converse, and his hands fucking ached with the desire to touch all that gorgeous exposed skin. Finally, he made it to Tara. "Congratulations, T. You deserve this."

She beamed up at him. "Thanks, Sean."

He switched places with Dani and shook hands with Jesse next. "New job. Getting married. Damn, Jesse. You're killing it, man."

Jesse laughed as he returned the shake. "Somehow I got really fucking lucky, is all."

Sean turned to make room for Dani to get to Tara and just caught Dani's expression—for a split second, she looked utterly wrecked. And then she smiled and hugged Tara tight.

"Wow, I'm so happy for you guys. Now how long have you two been keeping this from us?" Dani teased Tara.

Tara gave a coy grin. "I know. I'm sorry. We were going to share after WFC last week, but then the accident happened."

"Fine," Dani said teasingly, then gestured at Tara's hand. "Let me see this gorgeousness."

Tara held out the hand with the diamond. "Isn't it amazing?"

Dani grinned. "So amazing. You obviously have great taste, Jesse. In rings and women."

The man nodded and pulled Tara in against him. "All I know is there's no one else for me."

Sean felt like a total observer as this conversation unfolded. Normally, he would've rushed in to apologize that his unluckiness had interrupted the sharing of their happy moment, but he was still laser focused on what Dani's expression had meant. Especially when she held up her cell phone and said, "Oh, shit. I'm sorry. Hospital."

Except...from where he stood behind her, Sean saw that the screen remained blank. She hadn't received any calls or texts. He watched as she quickly threaded her way through the restaurant toward the bathrooms, his gut suddenly in knots for worrying about what was going on with her.

Not that it was his place, but fuck. He couldn't help it.

When the waiter dropped off their checks, Dani still hadn't returned, so he paid for both of theirs. Noah and Kristina reminded everyone of the details of next weekend's July 4th festivities, and then everyone was saying their good-byes. Afterwards, Sean went back to the bathrooms. Not sure what else to do, he knocked on the women's room door. "Dani?"

The door flew open, and there Dani stood, a total knock-out in that little skirt and Converse. "What the hell are you doing?"

"Looking for you. Everyone's leaving. You okay?" He studied her face. Beautiful as always, but something was off with her eyes, like she'd hung shutters in front of them and they didn't shine quite as bright.

"Yeah, of course. Just hospital bullshit. Let me go say good-bye."

Sean nodded and followed Dani back through the restaurant, but his internal bullshit alarm was blaring. He was, after all, the king of playing shit off. Like, if there was an Olympic event for playing shit off like it was nothing, he would be the all-time record holder. And he'd seen her phone.

Dani's expression morphed into happiness again as she saw Tara and gave her and Jesse another hug. Promises were made to hang out and shop and look for gowns together. And Sean might've almost believed that he was reading the whole thing wrong until, out in the parking garage, Tara turned to Dani one last time.

"Oh, I was going to wait, but I can't. Dani, will you be my maid of honor?"

Annnd there was that look in her eyes again—only darker. Her jaw dropped.

Lost in her excitement, Tara misinterpreted Dani's silence as maybe surprise or hesitance. "I know it's a lot to ask and that we've only known each other for a year but you know I love you and I can't think of anyone I'd want standing beside me more than you."

Dani blinked and pushed a smile onto her face. "Oh, my God, I can't believe you'd want *me*. But of course, I'll be your maid of honor. I'm stunned and honored."

Another round of hugs and happy exclamations ensued. Meanwhile, Sean was nearly itchy to get Dani out of there before she burst and unleashed whatever her real reactions were to all this.

Finally, it was just the two of them. "Come on, I'll drop you at home," Dani said as she crossed the parking garage toward her car.

"Want me to drive?" he asked, probably taking his life into his own hands.

She made a face at him. "Why?"

He held up his hands. "Just offering."

Sean eased into the car, expecting to hit his knees on the dash, but he found that the passenger seat was still pushed back from when he'd used it last week. He got hit with the sudden and fucking ridiculous feeling of *fitting in* to her life, even in this small way, which just showed how pathetic he was sometimes.

The ride back to his house was quiet, but not at all peaceful. Because he could feel Dani raging from where he sat. The car was nearly vibrating with her chaotic energy. Her knuckles were white where she gripped the steering wheel. Her jaw was clenched tight.

"What?" she bit out, glancing over to find him watching her.

"Just looking."

"Well, don't."

"Why not?" He wasn't sure why he was pushing her, but everything inside him wanted to—in every way he could.

"Because."

If he laughed, she was going to legit fuck him up. So he remained serious. "Not good enough. I like looking at you."

She huffed, but Sean *was* looking, so he didn't miss the tint of pink that climbed up her high cheekbones. Dani liked him looking whether she admitted it or not.

His cock stirred and he shifted in his seat. And let himself look his fill. At the small swell of her breasts under that tight little shirt. At how high up the black denim skirt rode on her thighs. At how fuckin' pretty she was.

Sean found himself wanting a thousand things as he took Daniela England in. He wanted to know why Jesse and Tara's engagement had so bothered her. He wanted to make her feel better. He wanted to let her take all that pent-up anger or angst or whatever it was out on him. He wanted to hold her—a strange urge for someone who found hugs odd and unfamiliar.

He wanted to be inside her. And then fall asleep with her in his arms and wake up only to slide inside her again.

Fuck. What was *all that* about?

Dani could've dropped him off on the street in front of his house, but instead she pulled around into his back yard and parked with the engine idling. He wasn't sure why she'd done that, but his cock thought it knew, apparently, which maybe explained why Sean was rock fuckin' hard.

They sat there for a long second. Neither of them speaking or moving. And all Sean could think of was how the last time something had been on her mind she'd told him, *"I just want to get out of my head..."*

He knew how that was. So just in case that was where she was now, he needed her to know. "My offer stands."

She looked at him, fierce and beautiful. "Your offer?"

"You can use me."

"Fuck off, Sean."

The ice in her tone hit him right in the chest. He was the one who'd pushed this seat back last week after all—there was no metaphor about life or invitation in that.

"All right, Dani." He pushed the door open and heaved himself out. Without looking back, he made for the house. Whatever she needed, she clearly didn't need it from him.

Sean wasn't sure why he'd expected anything else. His fire-fighting abilities aside, he'd rarely been anyone's solution to a problem. And once he'd even fucked firefighting up so thoroughly that all these years later he still dreamed about it like it happened yesterday.

Standing on his little back porch, he fished for his keys in his pocket, which was when he realized that he no longer heard the sound of Dani's car. Except, he also hadn't heard her back out.

Giving in to the pull between them, he looked back—and found her coming up the sidewalk. Straight for him.

CHAPTER THIRTEEN

As DANI WATCHED Sean walk up the path to his house, guilt swamped her. She hadn't meant to take the hurricane spinning inside her out on him. But she had—because he saw too much of her. Why did he have to see her the way he did? The *real* her. The one that was an utter mess inside. No one else had picked up on the way she'd freaked out at Tara and Jesse's news, yet she had no doubt that Sean Riddick had.

Dani's first reaction to her friends' announcement had been happiness. She knew how hard Jesse and Tara had fought to be together, and she was thrilled that they'd found their happily ever after.

But a split second later, Dani had been absolutely blind-sided with a roiling mess of sadness, grief, guilt, and anger. Not to mention jealousy—and wasn't that just awesome. Dani wasn't sure how she'd managed to act normal for even a second after the storm of emotion had hit, destroying the walls she'd been trying to build around everything she felt about the upcoming anniversary. Apparently putting on masks and burying herself in routines and applying the force of sheer willpower weren't enough to keep all that roiling emotion at bay.

It was just that, what Tara and Jesse were sharing...it was something she was never going to have again. Instead, all she had in front of her was a series of never-ending anniversaries marking all she'd lost. And the utter freaking finality and bleakness of that realization had nearly leveled Dani.

That she'd had even an iota of care for herself amid their wonderful news made her the shittiest of friends, and then she'd bitten Sean's head off to boot. Dani sighed, but it didn't take any of the weight off her shoulders.

Against the light of his back porch, Sean's big silhouette stood out. Masculine. Strong. Sexy.

Steady.

That was something else Dani hadn't realized about Sean Riddick. For all his smart-ass snarkiness, sarcasm, and joking around, Sean was steady. Dependable and reliable. There when you needed him. Willing to put others before himself. The first one to celebrate his friends' accomplishments. Always genuinely happy for the good things that happened to other people. And in those ways, he was, once again, more than she'd given him credit for.

Without thinking, she'd killed the engine and gotten out of the car. Debated for no more than half a second. Sean stopped before opening the back door, and then Dani was operating all on instinct.

She went after him.

As if they were magnets, his gaze cut to her, making her feel seen again.

"I'm sorry," she said.

"You don't owe me any apologies, D." Sean jingled the ring of keys in his hand.

"I do." She sighed.

"Wanna tell me what's wrong?"

"Sometimes the past..." She hadn't intended to stop there,

but she got tangled up in not wanting to tell him the specifics but wanting to tell him *something*.

"Yeah. I know all about that," he said, like she'd explained it in full detail.

Dani twisted the ring on her middle finger. "So anyway."

"You comin' in?" Sean pulled open the screen door and slid his key into the lock. The interior door swung inward. He flicked on the hall light.

Dani wanted to go in with him. She really wanted to. For all her what-were-they, should-she-be-doing-this back-and-forth, her desire for Sean was the one thing not in question. But she also didn't want to take advantage of him. Or take his head off again.

"You want me to?" she asked.

Leaning against the door jamb, Sean held the screen door open with one big boot. He'd gone casual tonight in a pair of well-worn jeans and a white button down cuffed at his forearms —and he looked like the orgasm-giving god he was, especially when he slanted her a look. "Did you just ask me if I wanted you to come in, or if I wanted you, also?"

Frowning, Dani's mouth dropped open and her brow cranked down. And then she realized what he was asking. Her words could've been interpreted either way: 'you want me to?' or 'you want me, too?'. And, now that she thought about it, she was curious to know the answer to both of those questions. So she simply said, "Yes."

Sean was in front of her in a second, dark eyes blazing. "Yes. I want you. And, yes, I want you to come in so I can show you how much."

Dani's heart was a sudden staccato drum beat in her chest. There was nothing casual about the tone in Sean's voice—raw, determined, even a bit commanding. "Okay."

He shook his head. "No. Give me more than that. You want me? Tonight? Now?"

"Yes."

"How?"

His sudden intensity unleashed a shiver over her skin. God, he hadn't even touched her and she was already on edge. "I want you inside me."

"Oh, you better fucking believe I'm gonna get inside you, Daniela. I want to know how you want it."

An image came to mind and she gave voice to it before she second-guessed herself. "Pull my skirt up and take me from behind."

The next thing Dani knew, she was over Sean's shoulder and being carried into the house. Up the stairs.

"Sean, put me down. You're gonna hurt yourself, you big idiot!" She tried to twist out of his hold, but his arm was tight around the backs of her legs.

"I'm fuckin' fine," he said in a sexy growl. "And we both know you like getting held down, so don't pretend that this isn't making you wet."

"Damn you," she said, dizzy more from the force of her arousal than hanging upside down.

He let out a sexy chuckle as he started up the stairs to his second floor. Her thinking brain wanted her to tell him he was going to hurt himself again, but she surrendered to the baser part of herself. The part that knew Sean was right.

She was already wet.

He dropped her unceremoniously on his big bed. The gray-and-white-striped sheets were messy, and the hunter green comforter was folded back, all as if Sean had just rolled out of bed. It made it feel more intimate, somehow, like she was seeing into a part of his life that she wasn't meant to see. She rolled to find Sean tearing the button-down off, exposing those muscled shoulders and ridged abdomen. His bruising wasn't quite as dark now, and in places was turning yellow-green as it healed.

Dani's gaze dropped down to the considerable bulge that filled out the front of his jeans. God, she wanted him to absolutely overwhelm her. And she knew he was one hundred percent capable of it, too.

From the nightstand, Sean withdrew a condom packet which he tossed on the edge of the bed. And then, as if he'd heard her thoughts, he proceeded to drive her right out of her mind.

Sean grasped her ankles and dragged her body toward him until she laid bent over the bed. And then he rucked up the soft denim of her mini-skirt, exposing her bare skin and the black lace of her thong.

"Fuck," Sean bit out as one hand stroked up her thigh to squeeze her ass. "You fantasized about me seeing you like this, didn't you? This gorgeous fuckin' ass up in the air, this lace taunting me to shred it."

"Yes," she said, because it was true. She'd picked out this thong with that exact errant dirty thought in mind. It would absolutely fall apart in his hands—if he wanted it to.

The thud of boots and the shifting of clothing sounded out from behind her, but the next thing Dani felt was not what she expected. Sean's big hands landed on her ass and spread her open, and then his mouth was all over every intimate part of her. Licking and tonguing her pussy, lapping at her clit, pushing into her rear and making her gasp and writhe. It'd been years since anyone had taken her there, but it had always driven her wild. And God but remembering how much she'd always loved being played with and fucked there ratcheted up her arousal, her lust, her need.

For Sean.

So damn quickly, Dani's body was shaking and trembling,

but she couldn't do anything to drive herself closer to orgasm because his big arms had her thighs pinned to the side of the bed, and his hands held her ass right where he wanted it, right where he had full access to every secret part of her. "*Sean*." She swallowed hard, so freaking needy. "Please."

There was a click and then something cool at her rear entrance. His fingers swirled in the slickness before one pushed inside her ass. "Please, what?" he asked. Not that he waited for her answer, because his mouth was back between her legs, licking and sucking and fucking her pussy with his tongue as his finger gently slid deeper into her rear.

Her hands fisted in the sheets. "Oh, Jesus fuck. Please make me come."

Teeth nipped at her ass. "Fuck, you beg so pretty."

"You'll not only say it, Dani. You'll beg me for it."

Dani groaned at the memory of his taunt and managed to rasp, "Don't get used to it."

Sean's chuckle was full of smug sin, but she could hardly complain about that when one of his hands forced her back to arch more, tilting her ass further up and allowing him to work the hard suction of his mouth around her clit. As he sucked her off, he flicked his tongue against her clit in a fast, maddening rhythm that had her holding her breath and straining. But it was him fucking her ass with that finger in a sudden fast in-and-out that had her tensing, then coming and coming, releasing a muffled scream against his bed that left her dizzy and floating.

She'd barely come down from the exquisite soaring high of her orgasm before Sean was easing his finger from her. A wrapper crinkled, and then the head of his cock was at her pussy, teasing and tormenting her as he let his length slide through the wetness he'd worked out of her.

"I fuckin' love the sound of you coming, Daniela. Makes me so hard." His cock penetrated her, letting her feel just how hard he was. And so thick that not a single part of her felt empty. Not a single one. And she could've cried from the goodness of it.

The rightness of it.

The I've-missed-this-so-much of it.

And she could've kissed him when he didn't give her a chance to think about those thoughts, because just then he grasped the now bunched-up mini-skirt around her waist and used it to pull her back to meet his demanding thrusts. Sean didn't build up to fucking her. No. He fucked her like he somehow knew she needed to be fucked. Hard. Demanding. Deep. Overwhelming in the most perfect of ways. All Dani could do was moan at the sheer pleasure coursing through her.

"Hands at your lower back," he growled, his hips slapping against her ass.

Electricity danced down Dani's spine as she did what he said. Anticipation flooded through her as one of his big hands pinned her wrists. She was well and truly held down. Totally under Sean's control. And it was freaking glorious.

Dani was the one using Sean, but she felt used in return. Not in a way that took advantage, but in a way that was about two people finding something they needed in someone else. Which was when Dani realized that she wanted Sean to find pleasure in her. Solace if he could. Distraction if that was what he needed.

All of it. She wanted him to find that in her. *With* her.

His thrusts filled her and rocked her body roughly against the messy covers, creating a delicious friction against her nipples and clit. She gave herself over to the pleasure and moaned at how good Sean felt. His hands at her wrists and using the skirt as if he was riding her. His big thighs colliding with the backs of her legs. His heat setting off a fire inside her.

When Dani could manage to think at all, she had flashes of their night. Of the way Sean had looked when he'd arrived at the restaurant. On the surface, he'd been his usual smiling, outgoing self. But exhaustion hung around his eyes. And he'd tuned so far out when they were ordering that he hadn't heard three of them saying his name.

An hour ago, she'd felt like utter spiraling shit, and somehow he'd managed to make her laugh, bring her comfort and understanding, and help her escape all the mess. Making it so that all she felt now was euphoria. Sheer and complete.

"Aw, fuckin' hell, Daniela," Sean groaned, the deep rumble of it licking up her spine. God, she liked knowing that she wrecked him, too.

"You gonna come inside me, Sean?" she said, peering over her shoulder.

As soon as their gazes met, Sean fell forward on top of her, his strong arms shifting her up the bed so that she was lying flat on her stomach and he was covering her from face to toes. "Fuck, Dani, take everything I got," he said, face to face with her. Eye to eye. Sensation tightened between her legs. But her reaction was even greater than that, because something in his words had her stomach fluttering, too. Like, maybe, he didn't just mean his orgasm. Like he meant something more.

"Did you just ask me if I wanted you to come in, or if I wanted you, also?"

He wanted her.

He wants me.

The fundamental truth of that cracked her right open.

She moaned as the orgasm rolled through her, and then lost her breath to his thoroughly claiming kiss. She didn't mind though because just then he groaned out her name and gripped her tight. She felt the jerk of his orgasm and the clench of his muscles everywhere. They shared panting breaths, lurid, drawn-out kisses, and lingering stares. Dani didn't think she was imagining the raw emotion in Sean's eyes.

The desire. The invitation. The hope.

And it was the hope that reached inside Dani's own chest and lit a spark that had been dark for years, that she thought would never bloom into embers or flames again. *Could never* even get ignited again.

Yet, as they lay there panting, his massive body still holding her down and making it hard to breathe, she couldn't find it in herself to smother that little flicker of light. Or to feel bad...for the first time in forever.

"Shit, sorry," he said, sliding to the side of her but not so far that they weren't still touching.

She shook her head against the sheets. "Don't apologize. Felt good."

A smile played around his lips and lit up those dark eyes. God, it took so little to please him, which made her realize how much he fed off of the smallest bits of praise. It made something squeeze in her chest, and maybe that was why she suggested it. "Should we continue the movie marathon?"

Sean's expression morphed from lazy masculine satisfaction to boyish delight in about two seconds. "Seriously? Hell, yes." He slid off the bed and stood in all his naked glory, one hand cupping at the condom and the other scratching at his bruised chest. "We're up to the second Thor movie."

Dani grinned and scooted to the edge of the bed. "Ooh, Thor."

He smirked and made for the bathroom, and she took full advantage of watching that ass in motion. Jesus. "Do you only like these movies for Captain America's ass and Thor's... hammer?" he asked from the bathroom doorway.

She retrieved her thong from the floor and made a show of sliding it back up her legs before she put her skirt to rights again. "I mean, that doesn't hurt. But, really, why would I need them when I have you right here in person?"

He stalked toward her, his expression so damn satisfied. "Is that right?" His hands settled possessively on her hips, and an arrogant smirk painted his lips—one that before might've irked her as much as it attracted her. Now she knew it was just a part of their give-and-take and that there was a whole lot more beneath the mask of arrogance that Sean Riddick sometimes wore.

"Of course," she said, feeling too soft and satisfied and uninhibited to hold anything back. "These movies are awesome, Sean. But you're the real thing."

CHAPTER FOURTEEN

A WEEK AGO, Sean had been body slammed by a truck and his world had been turned upside down. But standing there with Dani's praise hanging in the air between them, Sean felt like he'd been body slammed again.

In a good way. But one that still turned his world upside down.

Because he wasn't used to people thinking the best of him. Sure, he knew people liked him. And why not? He was a smart-ass motherfucker who knew how to have a good time and make people laugh. But that wasn't the same as being thought of as a fundamentally good person.

As being the real thing.

Especially after what he'd done.

Sean swallowed as he tried to think of a comeback. But Dani might as well have coldcocked him for how tongue-tied he was.

"Gotta use the bathroom. Meet you downstairs?" she asked, totally casual-like, but his gut told him she was also giving him a graceful out from this moment.

"Yeah," he managed, not letting go of her until he'd planted a kiss on her forehead. *Thank you*, he thought. But what he said was, "I'll go foraging for snacks."

She chuckled as she made for the bathroom.

He retrieved his boxers and jeans, liking the sound of Dani in his space. The vast majority of the time when he'd been with a woman, it was at her place. Only rarely had he brought someone home. And he couldn't even remember the last time. Sean hadn't thought he'd avoided that on purpose, but now he wondered. Maybe if he opened the door to having someone here, it would feel worse when he was alone again? Because having Dani here now? Hearing her moving around and sharing his space? It felt good. And he knew it was gonna suck when he got better and she wasn't coming around as much anymore.

Well maybe you should put yourself out there and let her know you'd like her to come around even after all this is over.

Fuck. Standing there staring off into space, he scrubbed a hand over his face.

Finally, he pulled an old, comfy T-shirt from a drawer and tugged it over his head, grimacing as his chest protested the movements. Dani hadn't been wrong—it *had* hurt to carry her up the steps. But the fact that she'd let him get away with doing it had been too fun for him to care. He'd withstand pain for her every fuckin' day if it meant that she'd be with him like this.

Something uncomfortable tweaked inside his chest that had nothing to do with the injury he'd sustained.

His head was in the pantry when she joined him in the kitchen.

"Tell me you have some snacks because I'm munchy now," she said.

"Oh, I got snacks all right," he said, pulling things out and setting them on the counter. "Pretzels, chips, some cheese popcorn but no more caramel." He held up a container of cashews. "Deez nuts."

Dani chuckled, and fuck she looked beautiful standing in his kitchen, her cheeks still a little flush, her lips soft and puffy from their kisses. "Yes to all of it."

"Good choice." He winked. "I made you work up an appetite, I see."

She rolled her eyes. "Whatever, Riddick. Sometimes a woman just needs snacks."

Sean grinned. No way was he buying that. "Uh huh. Suuure. Whatever you need to tell yourself, D."

Without missing a beat, she threw the container of nuts at him, and he burst out laughing despite the fact that he barely caught it before it nailed him in the chest.

Her eyes went wide. "Oh, my God, Sean. I'm so sorry. I wasn't thinking."

"You've got a fuckin' arm on you," he said, still chuckling and having no idea why she was apologizing.

"I'm really sorry."

Cashews now securely in hand, he grabbed two bottles of water for them. "Why are you apologizing?"

"Because if that had hit your chest, I would've really hurt you." Distress and regret were clear in her expression.

There she went again, knocking him flat on his ass. Just by caring. "Hey, I'm good. Okay? And we're good."

She twisted her lips. "No blood, no foul?"

He winked at her. "Exactly. Now, come on." They scooped up the buffet of snacks, made their way downstairs, and set everything out on the coffee table in the basement. Sean rubbed his hands together. "You're going to like this one."

"Is this our eighth movie?" she asked.

"Yep."

"And how many are there again?"

He slanted her a look. "Just go with the flow here, woman."

She laughed. "Just tell me."

At this point he wasn't telling her just for the fun of it because, unlike back at the beginning, he now believed she truly was interested and enjoying the movies. "No. I'm giving you Chris Hemsworth. Be grateful."

Giggling, she shook her head. "You know I could just Google it."

"Yes, but you won't or you would've done it by now." He pressed Play.

A few seconds later she whispered, "How many?"

"Sshh." He bit back a smile, but man he dug when they spent time together like this.

They both stretched for the popcorn at the same time, then they both sat back at the same time, and then they both reached again. "Oh my God, it's like we're teenagers. Here." She put the metal tin in the crook of her lap. "Now we can both reach it."

Sean gave her a look but couldn't hold back a smirky grin. "Are you inviting me to eat from between your legs?" He tossed a few kernels into his mouth.

Dani batted her lashes at him. "Sean Riddick, as good as your mouth is, you can eat from between my legs every day and twice on Sundays."

He nearly choked as he started coughing, and was both laughing and tearing up by the time she pushed a bottle of water into his hands and told him to drink.

"God, I'm going to kill you at this rate," she said, when he finally got himself under control.

Hugging a pillow to his chest, he managed a grin and a watery wink. "Yeah, but what a way to go."

Finally, they settled into actually watching the movie, and it was...strange how comfortable it was sitting there with Dani in his basement. Watching his favorite movies. Taking turns digging into the popcorn. It all felt oddly natural. Normal.

Temporary.

Which, given his track record, was probably better for her.

Sean sighed. All this churn in his head kept him from really enjoying the movie. He needed to go for a run. Or punch something. Or fight a goddamn fire.

But as none of those things were in his immediate future, he kept his ass planted right where it was. And then Dani grabbed a pillow, propped it against his thigh, and stretched out with her head leaning against him.

Her gaze cut up to his. Lingered for a moment. "You mind?"

"My leg is your leg," he said, not meaning to repeat that line but glad that he did when she chuckled.

"I'm wondering just how broadly this principle applies."

"How broadly would you like it to apply, Dani?"

What had he hoped for when he'd asked her that question? And why did it seem like that'd been months ago? A weird compression of time had happened since the accident, one defined by him spending way more time than usual within these four walls...and with Daniela England. And now he had an idea of how broadly *he* might like that principle of 'what was his was hers' to apply, but knew it was a pipe dream he shouldn't even waste his time thinking about.

She deserved more than his uncharmed life.

When the final scene faded off the screen, Sean said, "So what did you think?" Which was when he realized that Dani had fallen asleep. He rested his hand on her shoulder. "Hey, D?"

Nothing. She was out cold. The LED on the cable box read 12:35. Sean knew she didn't have to be to work until tomorrow evening, so he gently slid out from under the pillow, turned, and with a grimace he was glad she wasn't awake to see, he lifted her into his arms.

God, she felt so fuckin' good curled in against his chest.

He was carrying her up the basement steps when her eyes

open and gazed up at him all soft and warm. "You're carrying me again," she said in a voice that sounded half-asleep.

"Yep."

"Put me down," she said, her eyelids sagging.

He chuckled. "Okay."

"Mean it."

"I know."

By the time he'd made it back up to his bedroom, his chest was a three-alarm fire, but it was worth it when he laid her down on his bed.

She stretched. "I can go home."

Stay, he thought, liking the thought of her sleeping in his bed. Maybe too much. "It's late. Might as well sleep here."

"'kay." Her hands went to the button on her mini-skirt, and then she was clumsily pushing the denim over her hips. Damnit all to hell but he found it appealing not just because of how fuckin' gorgeous she was, but because the action wasn't sexual. It was just her getting comfortable for bed. And somehow that struck him as even more intimate.

He helped pull the covers up over her, then ducked into the bathroom. When he was finished there, he made for the door. "Night."

Dani pushed up onto an elbow. "Wait. Where are you going?"

"Oh, uh, downstairs. I figured...the couch."

"Stay." She flipped back the covers and scooted to the far side of his big bed.

Satisfaction jolted through Sean's gut. The repetition of the word he'd just thought had him crossing the room and getting into bed until they were laying on their sides facing each other. Staring at each other. Just an arm's reach apart.

"Can I ask you a question?" he said.

For a moment, hesitation played around those striking black eyes, but she finally nodded. "Sure."

"Why did you say you wished you'd known about superheroes when you were a kid?"

TWO REACTIONS COURSED THROUGH DANI— RELIEF that he hadn't asked why she'd been so upset at the restaurant, and uncertainty about how much to share in answer to the question he had asked. A third reaction followed close behind—appreciation. Appreciation that Sean had remembered what she'd said. Appreciation for the sincerity in his gaze as he lay there looking at her. Appreciation of the fact that something was happening between them—whether she knew what to do with that or not.

Life hadn't surprised her in a good way in a lot of years, and a part of her was opening to something she didn't truly understand. It made her feel good. It made her feel *better*. But why did feeling better have to come at once with a sort of shame. Like doing better was an affront to Anthony's memory.

So, fine, she wouldn't talk about Anthony. Not with another man. Not in that man's bed. Certainly not when she was so raw where her first love was concerned right now.

"Well," she finally began, "because it would've been nice to have been able to imagine there being heroes around who could save all the people I lost," she said. Outside of her family, Anthony was the only other person who ever knew all this about Dani, who knew how loss had shaped so much of her life.

Sean reached out, bridging the short distance between them and clasping Dani's hand in his. In her mind's eye, this man was always larger than life. His job. His usually gregarious personality. His sexuality and swagger. Who knew this sweet, soft, quiet side to him existed as well? And it made it easier for her to keep talking.

"My mom died when I was only two weeks old from complications of my birth, so I grew up with my dad and his parents, my nana and pap. I missed having a mom, but I also had a lot of love in my life. And I had Granny, my mom's mother, to tell me who my mama was and keep me connected to that whole side of the family. That was really important because my dad and his family were white, but my mama's people were members of the Kiowa tribe, and without Granny, I wouldn't have really had a way to learn about or be a part of that community."

"It keeps happening," Sean said, swallowing.

"What?"

"Finding things that we have in common. My mom died when I was really young, too. I was five, but my memories of her are pretty vague. More impressions or feelings than fully formed memories, if that makes sense."

"It does," she said, surprised to hear that Sean had apparently been noting all those commonalities just like she had. And this answered her question about what his mother had been like given that he'd described his dad as a "shit father". "Five is so young. I'm sorry. And you're right. It does keep happening, doesn't it?"

He nodded. "Tell me more."

Dani adjusted her head on the pillow and took a deep breath, because she really hadn't told him anything yet. "Granny knew everyone. She knew their business and she knew how to get shit done. She made sure people had food if they needed it. She made arrangements for people to go to the doctor if they needed to. She volunteered for everything and she was impossible to say no to, which made her highly effective at recruiting volunteers for absolutely everything."

"She sounds like a badass like you."

Dani grinned. "She definitely was. I come by my ball-busting naturally." She winked and loved that it made Sean chuckle. "She took me along to help out on everything she did. I served at the elders' Christmas dinner, sold raffle tickets at the annual summer festival, and helped deliver meals to people who couldn't get out and about. She took me to all the Pow Wows and made sure I attended the youth language and culture camps. My favorite thing, though, was the Black Leggings Warrior Society Ceremonial, a dance that recognizes the role of warriors and soldiers in the tribe and honors their contributions to the country. To young me it was so inspiring, because these were people who'd devoted their lives to serving other people, and that's what I wanted, too. It's part of what made me want to join the army."

"And what made you want to be a nurse?" Sean asked, like he was absolutely fascinated.

Dani's gaze dropped to where his thumb was lazily stroking across her knuckles. That little bit of connection felt so good. It was exactly the kind of thing she'd been missing for so long.

"Is this okay?" he asked, squeezing her hand.

"Yeah."

"Is this too weird?" he asked. "Us, being serious and talking about real stuff?"

There was a vulnerability in his eyes that told her how much this was meaning to him—and it made her realize it meant something to her, too. Whatever this was, they were in it together. "If it's weird at all, it's good weird."

He quirked a lopsided grin. "Good weird kinda describes us, don't you think? 'Your crazy matches my crazy. Big time.'"

She laughed at the line from 'Deadpool'. "Apparently so," she said, squeezing his hand. And then she sighed, because she was at the hard part of her story now.

"You don't have to answer my question if you don't want to," he said, giving her an out.

But she wanted to tell him. "No, it's okay. I haven't talked about any of this in a really long time, and it's nice. I became a nurse because my father died in a construction accident when I was eight. It took the ambulance twenty minutes to arrive. I was with Granny when we heard about it, and we were close enough that she drove us there. She knew the foreman, and he took one look at me and wouldn't let us get closer. My dad was bleeding out no matter what they did, and he didn't want me to see him that way. But I wanted nothing more than to go to him. To help him. And that was the day I decided, whatever I did with my life, I would help people."

Sean frowned, and the concern was plain in his gaze. "What happened to you after your dad died?"

"My dad and I had lived with his parents my whole life already, so my grandparents raised me. I had it better than a lot of kids in that situation. I still had family."

"Doesn't mean it was easy, I bet," he said, his voice gentle.

"No," she said. "After that, it was seeing my granny struggle with her diabetes that made me wish even more that I had medical knowledge. And it wasn't just her, either. Diabetes is basically an epidemic among native communities. Granny died from complications of it when I was fifteen. With her gone, I lost a lot of my connection to the tribe because Nana and Pap weren't very able to get around and take me places, and my ancestry didn't qualify me for official enrollment in the tribe anyway. All of that made high school interesting. It was hard sometimes to figure out who I was and who I wanted to be with my parents gone and my feet partly in two worlds. So I just buried my nose in books and put all my focus into doing well in school so I could get a ROTC scholarship for the nurse training program."

Sean gave her a good, long look. "That's a lot of loss for such a young person. No wonder you're so damn strong."

At once, Dani felt warmed by the praise and like such a fake, because, well... "I don't feel so damn strong."

"Nobody feels strong all the time, right? But the fact that they put one foot in front of the other and keep fuckin' going is what matters. That's strength personified."

She blinked at his choice of words, and then she held up her left hand to show him the tattoo on her finger.

"What the shit?" he said, chuckling. "Oh. I thought you were flippin' me off for a sec there." He took her hand in his much bigger one. "K.F.G. Look at that. See? It's in your very skin, D."

"You're a good guy, Sean," was all Dani could say to that, because there was suddenly a lump in her throat. One that wasn't so much about grief as it was about feeling seen for the first time in so long. Damn him.

He winked. "Don't tell anyone."

She smirked. "I won't."

"I'm glad you stayed, Daniela," he said, piercing into her with those dark eyes.

"So am I."

"Should we get some sleep?"

It was the first time she'd talked about any of this in years, and it had left her lighter but exhausted. "I guess we should."

"'kay." He reached back and clicked off the lamp. "Night, D."

Dani reveled at the deep rumble of his voice in the dark, at the connection of their hands as he laced their fingers together. "Night, Sean."

It had been so long since she'd slept with another person that, for the longest time, she couldn't drop off to sleep. Her brain held her there, suspended in the feeling, not, for once, of solitude, but of...togetherness. And Sean Riddick—of all people —had given that to her after so very long.

Dani waited for the feeling of shame to wash over her for so enjoying it, but it didn't come.

And then she was able, finally, to fall asleep.

CHAPTER FIFTEEN

It started the way it always did, with the bells.

Sean hadn't been asleep for more than fifteen minutes. He'd just racked out after a fourteen-hour shift when the constant buzzing went off and he was up again.

But that's how it was when you were a Damage Control-man. There wasn't anyone else, and it was your home that was burning down. Fire was one of the biggest threats sailors faced at sea, which made firefighting—just one of the controlmen's jobs—among the most important.

The question was, what kind of fire waited for him? He wouldn't know that until they were standing in front of the beast itself, heat blasting them in the face, smoke threatening to crawl down their throats. The haze of it already hung in the air.

In less than a minute he was in the DC Unit Locker Room and gearing up.

As the fire marshal, Senior Chief Ortez had already donned his bunker gear and protective equipment. "Tonight, Chief Riddick is our on-scene leader and Petty Officer Roberts our team leader. I'll see you down there," he said, heading out first to make an initial assessment.

"Did you feel it?" Emerson asked when the senior chief departed.

Sean frowned as everyone began recounting what they felt and what they'd been doing when they felt it. The long and short of it was that a big-ass shudder had rocked through the destroyer seconds before the bells sounded.

"Shit, seriously? I was out cold," Sean said.

"Damn, Chief, you could sleep through World War III," Westover said.

"Hey, it takes a lot of shut-eye to look this good," Sean retorted, glad for the joking and camaraderie. Tension was clear on the faces of the new guys who had joined them only three weeks before. Of course, they'd been trained within an inch of their lives and had run countless drills, but you never knew how anyone would react until they were in front of the fire with flames shooting out at them. Even with all the training, you couldn't fully know the heat of the real thing until you were in front of it, and you couldn't know who might panic when the chips were down.

Petty Officers 1st Class Roberts and Khan double checked that all the newbies were kitted-up correctly and gave Sean a nod when they were satisfied.

"Good. Now let's go put the wet stuff on the hot stuff, boys and girls," he said before securing the face shield to his oxygen breathing apparatus. They double-timed it through the ship's narrow decks and hatches, the general announcing system blaring a warning about the fire, until they finally reached the aft engine rooms.

And that's where they found the enemy.

Sean's mind cleared of everything except fighting the fire. He turned to his team. "It's showtime, people," he said through the voice amplifier on his mask. "We find and evacuate victims, analyze the nature and spread of the fire, remove any combustibles, and get it nice and wet. Heads in the game. Let's go."

He and his team poured into one of several connected compartments where the main propulsion systems, boilers, generators, and auxiliary machinery were located, the first of the DC-men fanning out to conduct search and rescue, the ones coming in next continuing on. The smoke was thicker here but at least the fire hadn't spread this far.

Leaving a few of the others to complete a sweep of that space, he led a group into the next compartment. Sean nearly tripped over a sailor sprawled across the floor. "We've got a vic here," he called, stepping out of the way so that the others could clear the hatch while he knelt to assess the sailor, who had burns on his face, arms, and hands. At Sean's touch, the guy's eyes rolled open and he mumbled something Sean couldn't make out. "Hang in there, seaman." Sean peered over his shoulder. "Keaton, over here."

Flames crawled through the far hatch and up the bulkhead.

Ah, so there it was—the boundary of the fire. Now they just needed to keep it there. *I'm coming for you, motherfucker*, he thought.

"What do you need, Chief?" Keaton asked. He was one of the newbies and assigned to first aid for this incident.

"Get him out to the passageway," Sean said, waving over another of the men on first aid duty.

Sean hustled further in, passing two more victims who were already being assisted, and crossed into the fire zone in the third compartment, which was where things got dicey. They had a Bravo fire on their hands, which referred to the combustible liquid fire roaring in front of them from what appeared to be leaking fuel oil. The heat was so intense he could feel it through his gear.

Taking a further moment to assess the extent of the fire, he rounded the wreckage of equipment to see a gaping hole pouring out thick smoke and flames into the room. This was likely the source of the shudder that apparently everyone else on the ship had felt except him. And what he saw here was bad news. Leaks were spraying out and catching fire, turning into a spray fire that meant—*fuck a duck*—that this mofo wanted to spread.

"Get two lines going," he shouted to his team leader, who directed the nozzlemen and hosemen into position. When they had the hoses manned and pumping water into the heart of it, Sean kept a close eye on the teams and stepped in to advise the nozzleman working the spray fire on where to best focus to try to rein this bitch in. The last thing they wanted was to lose control of it, and Bravo fires were notoriously volatile. Using his wireless comms, he called in an initial report regarding the location and nature of the damage to the fire marshal and Damage Control Central.

Beneath some debris, Sean spotted another victim. Carefully, he lifted off pieces of metal to free the man. Suddenly, Keaton was right by his side and lending a hand, and then they were joined by Jackson, one of his most experienced controlmen. The unconscious sailor had burns all down his front, but what worried Sean was the impact injuries they couldn't see.

"I'll go get a spine board," Keaton called out over the roar of the hoses and the flames, but before Sean could respond, he was already taking off. Sean appreciated the kid's quick response and initiative, because his gut was telling him they might not have much time.

Jackson gave him a look that said she knew it, too. "I can handle this from here, Chief."

Nodding, he made for the guys manning the hose. Their efforts were just barely keeping the fire on the liquid pool side under control, but despite all the water they were shooting at this sucker, the spray fire appeared pretty damn close to a lost cause. He watched them work for a few more minutes when the smoke and flames cleared just long enough for him to spot several oil drums lined up against the far bulkhead. And that was when he decided that shit was about to get critical.

They had a major combustible risk. It was time to pull out.

He went to both teams and gestured toward the door. "Pull out. We're initiating the Halon system." They evacuated the compartment and backtracked the way they'd entered, the boundarymen spraying down the bulkheads as they went and securing each of the hatches to create an air-tight seal. Back in the cooler passageway, Sean made sure everyone was out before the final door was closed, then he met the senior chief at the actuation station and advised him of the situation.

His superior agreed with Sean's assessment and immediately engaged the switch that shut down the ventilation fans to the affected compartments and initiated the Halon system, which used a combination of liquids and gases to suppress fire. A warning horn sounded immediately, and a sixty-second countdown began that gave anyone in harm's way time to evacuate.

It should've all been good from there, but instead, it was where shit started to go sideways.

Just then, word came through Sean's earpiece that the initial explosion had apparently ignited an electrical fire in the maintenance compartment below where they'd been working.

"How do you want to handle it, Chief Riddick?" his senior chief asked.

He appreciated the trust and confidence the question represented. So Sean continued to take charge. Using his wireless comms, he called for back-up personnel and then divided his team into two until that back-up arrived.

"Keaton, Westover, you're on reflash watch," Sean said to

two of his newbies before issuing commands to others that he no longer remembered. Because those turned out to be the only two that mattered...

Then he and the rest of the team descended one more deck to assess and contain the electrical fire. It was a nasty bitch of a fire, too. Charlie fires always were. And it was already threatening to get out of control. Luckily, no one had been injured here, so after assessing the fire, the extent of the damage, and in consultation with one of the electrical specialists, he made the call to engage the Halon system here, too.

He was just feeling good about getting things under control in relatively short order when another explosion rattled the ship.

What the fuck was that?

The public address system crackled on, announcing the locations of the fires and directing all hands to their stations.

Then DC Central was in his ear with the news that would change his life: there'd been a massive reflash event on the deck above resulting in multiple casualties.

Sean hauled ass up the ladder and through the passageways, the weight of his gear and the air tank on his back making him feel like he was running through molasses. One refrain ran through his mind: *Don't let it be Keaton and Westover.*

Oh, Jesus, don't let it be my guys.

CHAPTER SIXTEEN

"No! Nonono..."

The mournful shout jolted Dani awake. Blinking into the darkness, she was disoriented, but then Sean's pained voice reminded her where she was.

And, oh, God, she'd never heard him in so much pain, not even once after he got hit. His whole body shuddered.

Dani moved closer and laid a hand on Sean's chest. Beneath her palm, his T-shirt was damp and his heart was pounding so hard it was as if he were running. "Sean," she said, gently shaking him—which wasn't easy given how tense every muscle in his body was. "Sean, hey. Wake up."

"God, no," he rasped.

The sound of his voice made Dani's heart ache. In the hospital, she'd written off the bad dream he'd had as being a result of the accident, but this seemed like something else altogether. "Sean, it's me, Dani. Wake up."

His head jolted off the pillow. "What? What's wrong?"

"Hey, it's okay. You were having a nightmare. I'm sorry I woke you, but it seemed bad." She couldn't make out his expression as he dropped his head heavily and scrubbed a hand over his face, but with the other hand he covered hers where it rested on his chest.

On a long sigh, he released a single word, "Fuuuck."

Dani wasn't sure whether or not to push, but he'd been there for her earlier in the night when she talked about all her losses—okay, well, not Anthony—but all the rest. She could be here for him for whatever this was. So into the quiet of the room she asked, "Wanna tell me about it?"

A long moment passed before he finally said, "Gimme a sec." Then he slid off the bed and padded to the bathroom. The light of the bathroom made her realize he still wore his jeans, and then the door clicked shut behind him. It seemed a long time before he returned, now wearing a pair of boxers and a different T-shirt. He sat on the edge of the bed with his head hanging on his shoulders.

Dani hated the defeated cast of his body language. Whatever this was, he needed to fight it. And something inside her said he needed her help to do it. Which was why she closed the distance between them and hugged him from behind, her knees on either side of his hips, her body fitted against his back, her head on his shoulder, and her arms gently wrapped around him. "I'm listening if you need to vomit out whatever that dream was about."

There was a soft rumble that was almost a chuckle. "Vomit is about right."

"I'm worried about you. I'd hug you harder but I don't want to hurt you," she said, the darkness making it easier to voice the affection she felt towards him. The protectiveness. Exactly when had those feelings started?

"That's okay. I've never been much of a hugger anyway."

"Oh," she said, loosening her grip. "Should I—"

"*No.*" He caught her arms and encouraged her to hug him again. "I like this. It's not that I'm not into hugs, it's just that..."

Dani's belly had a sinking sensation because it seemed like whatever he was trying to say was rough, and she really wanted him to finish that thought.

"I guess it's just that, well, I didn't grow up with anyone ever hugging me, so it's a sensation I'm not used to is all. Shit." He groaned low in his throat.

Now her belly did a full-on free fall. No one *ever* hugged him? What a fucking asshole his father was. She had half a mind to drive to Philly and tell the elder Riddick to go fuck himself with a cactus.

"That's a real fuckin' sexy thing to admit, huh?" he said, his voice low in the darkness.

Dani snuggled in against his back and moved her mouth closer to his ear. God, he felt really damn good, all big and muscular against her. Sean Riddick had no problems where being sexy was concerned. But she decided to play this another way. "Look, I just want to get to know the real you. Not the short, two-dimensional sex object peddled by Hollywood."

If his chuckle was anything to go by, the 'Deadpool' line worked. "How do you know so many quotes from the movie already?"

Oh, boy, he was going to love this. "Well, I googled funny lines so I could text them to you the other day, and then I got myself hooked and had to watch it again."

He peered at her over his shoulder. "You watched 'Deadpool' again already? Without me?"

"Guilty," she said, hiding her grin against his muscled shoulder.

"On the one hand, respect. On the other, from now on, that's an us thing." The tone in his voice was all teasing, but Dani's mind threatened to get all spun up on the idea of anything being reserved as an *us thing*. Even though—damnit she was a contradictory mess!—it was kinda sweet at the same time.

"Think so, huh?"

"Know so," he said, facing away again. He shook his head. "Watching 'Deadpool' without me."

She couldn't help but smile. More than that, Sean made it *easy* to smile. When was the last time she could say that about anyone or anything? It wasn't like Dani walked around unhappy all the time. It wasn't that at all. It was that Sean...well, it was like he turned up the dial on her life, making everything brighter and bolder and funnier and sexier.

And that realization made a headache bloom behind her eyes. The damn anniversary was only three days away now—or it would be come morning—and she clearly needed to take some time to deal with her feelings around that whole situation.

In her gut, she knew what the problem was—a letter she'd had in her possession for six years but never opened. Come July, every year, she had to grapple with whether or not this would be the year she read what was inside of it. And the weight of that decision after all this time lanced dread through her veins.

"So the nightmare," Sean said, pulling Dani from her spiraling thoughts. She lightly rubbed his chest to let him know she was listening. "It's pretty much the same one every time, which makes sense since it's not so much a nightmare as it is a memory—a memory of the biggest mistake of my life, one that ended up killing two good men."

"What happened?"

For the next ten minutes, he spoke in a monotone, describing how he was the leader of a firefighting team battling a shipboard machinery explosion that spread to neighboring compartments and then erupted into a raging inferno when part of the fire reignited.

"It took us seven hours to contain and finally suppress the

fire," Sean said. "Two died. Eleven were injured. The damage was so extensive that the ship was forced to return to port in order to complete repairs. And a fuck-ton of that—including those deaths—was my fault. So, no superhero over here, in case that much wasn't already crystal fuckin' clear."

Dani really wished she could see his face so that he could read the sincerity on hers. But she stayed right where she was. "That's a terrible tragedy, Sean. I'm really sorry that happened. But how could a machinery explosion be your fault?"

He shook his head. "Not that part, thank fuck for small favors. But it was my call to station two newbies who'd been on the job a grand total of three weeks on reflash watch. Somehow, there was confusion about how long had passed since the fire suppression system had been deployed, and someone opened the sealed door to the compartment too soon and without running all the necessary safety checks. That made the still-hot materials reignite in a massive fireball that killed my guys instantly. Somewhere along the way, I fucked up in preparing them to do their jobs. Maybe I joked around with my team too much and somehow communicated that people didn't need to take things seriously. I don't know. Andrew Keaton and Billy Westover were their names. Nineteen and twenty-one years old. They were fuckin' kids."

"Jesus, Sean, I'm sorry. That's so damn young. But I know enough about damage controlmen to know your training is really extensive. You were right to trust them to be able to handle the job."

A sound like a growl rumbled in his throat. "Obviously I wasn't."

"Do you know why someone went back in that compartment the way they did?" she asked.

He heaved a breath. "All the investigation could find out was that Westover opened the door at eighteen minutes past deployment of the Halon system. Twenty to thirty is standard minimum. Keaton was phoning in a message that got cut off when the explosion happened, but he didn't have a chance to say anything that explained what happened." A long pause. "And the not knowing has eaten at me every day since."

God, did Dani understand that. "Whatever happened, Sean, it wasn't your fault." He scoffed, which wasn't altogether unexpected, so Dani pushed on. "Did the investigation determine that your performance was faulty in any way?"

Silence. Dani immediately knew they hadn't. "Is that a no?" she finally asked.

"Shut up," he said.

The quick retort made her smile, but it slipped back off her face as fast as it had come. Because it was entirely clear now that Sean used humor to distract from hard or painful things. And since he was funny and snarky and sarcastic a lot of the time, she couldn't help but wonder how often he might've put on a fun or funny demeanor to avoid things getting too real.

"What happened was terrible. I understand why you would feel guilty about what happened to your men. That's natural to an extent. And trust me that I understand questioning why you survive when people around you die. But feeling bad or sad isn't the same thing as being at fault. You didn't kill those men, Sean. The fire did. An unfortunate mistake did. A young sailor who didn't follow protocol did. But not you." Dani waited for him to push back again.

Instead, he turned in her arms, both of them shifting until they sat facing each other. After sitting and talking for so long, her eyes had adjusted to the darkness, and she could make out the contours of his ruggedly handsome face. How had she so badly missed the depths of this beautiful man?

"You don't think...less of me for knowing what I, er, what happened? Because I don't think too much of myself for it. I seem to have a shitty track record of hurting people I care about —my guys, my mother, you."

Dani was nearly dizzy with all the things that needed unpacked in that sentence—or maybe it was just the headache making her feel that way. "Of course I don't think less of you. What I just heard is that you were a skilled, trusted, and well-liked leader with a deep sense of duty who really cared about the men and women who worked under him. And what I see of the man sitting in front of me is someone who is compassionate and sensitive, who has somehow been made to feel like he has to shoulder the blame for things that weren't ever his fault. We already dealt with the question of you hurting me—you didn't. I wasn't paying enough attention, lifted my elbow away from protecting my side, and didn't defend myself the way I should have. So that settles that. Now how are you supposed to have hurt your mother before you were even five years old?"

"You're tough, you know that?"

"Damn straight. Now spill."

Seam chuffed out a small laugh and smirked. "Ballbuster," he murmured under his breath. She rolled her eyes. And then his expression got serious again. "My father said it was my fault that she had depression and drank. Neither started until after I was born, apparently, which made them my fault. And then she died of alcohol poisoning, which my father—"

"Your *shitty* father," Dani interrupted, seething at the abuse that man had heaped on little Sean.

"—yeah. Definitely shitty. He said I killed her. That she was fine before I was born. That *they* were fine before I was born. And then I ruined it all. Just by, you know, existing."

Dani gasped, and she felt heat crawl up her face. "What a fucking abusive asshole. Seriously, a cactus might be too good for him."

Sean tilted his head. "A cactus?"

She waved a hand. "Oh, nothing, I was just thinking earlier that I should ride to Philly and tell him to go fuck himself with a cactus."

"Ouch." A smile played around his lips. "They come in all sizes, you know, so surely there's a size that would be punishment enough."

She frowned at Sean's humor. "No, there wouldn't be. What he said to you was outrageously inappropriate, Sean. It was abusive and it wasn't true. Set aside for a moment the fact that you didn't ask them to fuck and you didn't ask to be born—those were their decisions—but you were a tiny, defenseless kid and he deprived you of love and comfort and security and that is so fucking wrong I could scream."

Sean kissed her. Just a soft brush of his lips against hers. And then he paused there until she leaned in to ask for more. By the time they came up for air, she was straddling his lap and his hands were in her hair.

"I don't think anyone has ever stood up for me like that before," he said, his voice a deep rumble.

"Well, you can count on me to do it as much as you need from now on," she said, making a promise that she didn't fully understand the contours of. How could this sentiment feel so right and so wrong at the same time? She rested her forehead against his.

"I'm feeling kinda glad that truck hit me," he said, "'cause you wouldn't be sitting here in my arms if it hadn't." For once, his tone was entirely serious, so this wasn't him trying to deflect with humor.

She took his face in her hands. "Riddick, I will never feel grateful about you getting hurt, but I am grateful that something pushed us past all the frenemies B.S. so that I could be sitting here in your arms right now."

This time when they kissed, it stayed soft and sweet. "I'm sorry I woke you up," he said, kissing her again.

"I'm not."

"Think you can get back to sleep again?"

"Yeah, probably," she said.

They moved to get under the covers, but this time he held out an arm, inviting her to snuggle in. She accepted the invitation, fitting herself in against the side of his big body. When he wrapped his arm around her shoulders and pulled her tighter, Dani could've cried at how good it felt—both because it'd been so long since she'd last been held this way, and because she imagined embracing like this wasn't something Sean was used to doing.

So she lifted a knee atop his thigh and pressed her face into crook of his neck to give him the full snuggling experience. If you were going to do something, you might as well do it right.

"Mmm." The appreciative sound came from deep in his throat. "Night, D."

"Night, Sean."

Now, Dani just had to decide, was this going to become an *us thing*, too?

CHAPTER SEVENTEEN

SEAN WOKE UP WITH A SMILE, which was not a thing that usually happened. But it dropped back off his sleepy face the second he realized Daniela wasn't still with him in his bed.

Fuck, had she left in the middle of the night? His gut was saying no way, but that old sabotaging part of his brain was saying *she probably ran as fast as she fuckin' could, sucka!*

He shifted onto one elbow. "Daniela?"

"Sean."

The voice was no more than a croak, and it was coming... from under his bed. "What the shit?" He peered over the edge—and found Daniela laying in a ball on the carpet wearing only her T-shirt and thong. "Why are you on the floor? How long have you been down there?" He was off the bed and kneeling next to her in an instant.

"Not long," she said. "I'm sorry I had to wake you up again."

Frowning, he brushed the hair back off her face. "Never apologize for needing me, Dani. Fuck, you're burning up." He cupped his hand against her forehead.

"Are you saying I'm hot?" she asked weakly, not quite managing a smile.

"You know that shit is true," he said, not feeling up to joking around when her skin felt so scarily warm.

"I was making my way back from the bathroom when nausea and dizziness hit me so hard I wasn't sure if I was going to throw up or pass out. And...uh, oh God," she put her hand to her mouth.

Sean bolted to the bathroom, grabbed the trash can, and returned to her. "Here."

Dani curled over it, and Sean felt so damn bad for her. He scooped her hair into one hand and held it back as she puked. "I'm sorry," she whispered.

"Don't you worry about a thing, D. Whatever you need."

She peered up at him, her face ashen. "I think it's passed for now."

"Think you could get into bed?" he asked.

"Maybe?"

"Come on." He nearly lifted her himself when she proved a little shaky. She groaned and pressed a hand to her head. "Hurting?"

"Yeah," she said, crawling into his spot. Laying on her side, she drew her knees up until she was in a tight ball.

"I have Tylenol and Aleve. Preference?"

"Better go with Tylenol with my belly feeling like this," she said, her eyes glassy.

"Okay. You rest. Be right back." He scooped up the trash can to clean out. Sean's gut was a knot of concern as he did that then found the Tylenol and a thermometer in his bathroom medicine cabinet. He filled a cup with water, rushed back to her, and settled on the edge of the bed. "Here you go."

Dani lifted her head enough to swallow. "Thank you."

"Open your mouth," he said. He pushed the button on the digital thermometer, and she complied immediately. He smirked. "Remind me to tell you to do that under different circumstances."

She managed a weak guffaw. "Keep dreaming, Riddick."

"Sshh. Take your temp, woman."

"So bossy."

"You and I both know you like my bossy side." He nailed her with a stare. "Now put that in your mouth before I hold you down and make you."

"I'm mildly aroused right now," she mumbled around the thermometer while fighting a grin.

"Jesus," he said, enjoying talking to her. Liking being able to take care of her even though he hated that she didn't feel good. And that made him think about the conversation they'd had in the middle of the night. He wasn't sure he'd ever talked to another living soul about his mother, but it just felt so...easy with Dani. And God, the way she'd fought with him—fought *for* him—when he'd told her about the fire and how he felt he'd failed his team. It'd knocked his world off its axis a bit if he was being honest.

Which was when realization hit him over the head even harder than that truck had managed to do—he had feelings for Dani. His gut checked that assessment and decided that wasn't stating the case strongly enough. He didn't just have feelings, he...loved Daniela England.

No, he was *in love* with her.

Jesus Christ, he was in love. For the first time in his whole fuckin' life. He was in love with this gorgeous, brilliant, brave, caring, fierce, ball-busting woman. Now what was he going to do about that?

Beeping interrupted his thoughts. "One-oh-two-point-one. Not terrible."

"Uh, that's pretty terrible in my book, D," he said, head

kinda spinning from worry and love. Apparently. "You rest for a while. I'll be back in a few."

"Why don't you take me home so I don't get you sick, too?" she said.

"Fuck that, D. If you really think you can make the trip home and you'd be more comfortable at your own place, I'll take you. But I'll be staying. No way I'm leaving you alone right now." He nailed her with a stare, a fierce feeling of protectiveness roaring through him. Damn. Was this what love felt like? 'Cause right about now he'd do anything to make Dani feel better, to make sure she was okay.

Shit, she had to be okay.

She put her hand on his. "No, you're right. I'll stay."

He was too concerned to even make a joke of her saying he was right. "Good. Okay. Hang tight."

"I'll be here."

Right where I want you to be. But he just nodded and made for the door. Downstairs in the kitchen, he debated what to do. Was it 'feed a fever, starve a cold' or 'feed a cold, starve a fever'? Fuck if he knew. So he googled that shit to learn that the medieval dude who came up with that saying in the first place was talking out of his ass. So, feeding was fine. Now, what did he have that might work for how Dani was feeling.

Rummaging through his pantry and fridge, he began pulling things out onto the counter. Saltine crackers, a banana, bottles of water and Gatorade. He also had a few popsicles left. From the laundry room, he grabbed a washcloth that he soaked with cold water. And then he remembered the bottle of Pepto in the junk drawer and added that to the mix, too. What else? He grabbed a big glass and filled it with crushed ice from the dispenser on the fridge door. Nodding, he surveyed the situation. He needed a way to carry all this up there. He snapped his fingers, opened the cabinet by the stove, and grabbed a cookie sheet. When it was loaded up, he made his way upstairs.

Back in the bedroom, he moved as quietly as he could even though cookie sheets seemed to amplify every fuckin' little noise. But no matter because Dani was still awake.

"Hey," she said.

"Hey. I brought provisions." He pushed the clock and lamp on the nightstand to make room for his makeshift tray.

"Did you bake me cookies?" she asked, smirking. Which at least was a sign of her normal self.

Sean arched an eyebrow. "No, ball-buster. I improvised. Now, what would you like?"

Chuckling, Dani propped herself up a little. "Looks like you thought of everything. Let me try the ice and see if that will stay down." He handed her the cup of ice and a spoon, too. "Aw, you even brought a spoon? That's so thoughtful." She looked at the spoon for an oddly long moment before she finally took a bite of the ice.

"I didn't know if you'd be able to lift your head enough to eat them right out of the cup," he said, hovering by the side of the bed and wanting to do something more.

"Sit down with me."

He grabbed the cold washcloth and sat. "I brought this for your forehead. And there's Pepto if you think that'll help."

She situated the folded cloth and took another bite of ice. It was strange seeing Dani down for the count like this, and Sean really hated it. It was so damn wrong.

"That feels good, thanks. Hey, what flavor are the popsicles?"

"Red and orange," he said.

She laughed weakly. "Red isn't a flavor."

He smirked. "Red is too a flavor and it happens to be my second favorite so you should feel honored."

"What's your first favorite?" Dani asked around another bite of ice.

"Purple. Grape. Whatev. I ate those first and they were all gone or I would've shared."

"I definitely feel honored."

"Shut up."

She softly smacked his leg. "I was being serious." Her black hair was mussed and her face was flush, but she was smiling up at him like he mattered to her and it made her the most gorgeous woman he'd ever known.

Damn it all to hell he fuckin' loved her.

The feeling was like a pressure in his chest, one that demanded release. But he wasn't saying a word right now, not while she wasn't herself. Because he had no clue how she was going to react. Them joking about 'Deadpool' being an "us thing" didn't mean they were in a relationship, after all.

You can count on me to stand up for you as much as you need from now on...

Her words from last night rang in his head. God, they'd meant so much to him. Still did. Sean almost couldn't imagine what life would be like to have someone like Daniela England at his side, *on* his side. And, oh, Jesus, in his fuckin' bed. The two of them against the world. Yeah, that was a kind of life he'd never even let himself imagine—one he would've said he didn't deserve and couldn't have anyway 'cause he'd just fuck it up. But her words had him believing that something else could be possible for him. Her words had him believing in himself for maybe the first time ever.

"What are you thinking about?" Dani asked, shifting to sit up a little.

"You." When her eyebrows raised, he added, "Just worried about you and want you to feel better."

She put her hand on his thigh. "You're really sweet, Sean. Thank you."

"Yeah, o'course," he said, feeling sorta awkward and self-conscious. Was that love, too? Because if so it was fuckin' ridiculous. "Anyway, it's the least I can do after you took care of me."

"I never minded," she said. "I've enjoyed hanging out."

Damn he liked hearing her say that. "Same, D." They looked at each other, their gazes direct, open, and it felt like something important hung there between them. But Sean wasn't sure how to broach it. So instead he asked, "Think you can handle a popsicle?"

Dani smiled. "I'm gonna tempt fate and try one. I need something with some flavor in my mouth."

A smile he couldn't resist started to twist at his lips, and she gave him a droll stare. "Aw, come on, D. If you're gonna throw me a softball like that, what d'ya expect me to do? Innuendo is my middle name."

"Relentless is your middle name," she said, chuckling and shaking her head. "Can I have an orange one, please?"

"You really can have the red," he said, tearing the wrapper open so the stick stuck out.

"No, the orange ones are my favorite, so I'm good with that. Also, grape is my least favorite." She took a long lick of it.

His brain shorted out for a second watching her tongue. "Uh."

"This is turning you on, isn't it?"

"Uh huh," he managed. She sucked the pop into her mouth. He blinked.

"There's literally no way to eat these that isn't suggestive," she said, giving him a look.

"I know," he said, grinning. "Me likey." She rolled her eyes, making him grin wider. "Also, I think our flavor preferences make us a good pair because we don't have to compete for our favorites and then we can share the reds."

Dani chuckled. "You've got this all figured out, don't ya?"

Not even a little bit, but fuck, he was willing to. With her. "Dude, if we can agree on popsicles, mixing the cheese and caramel popcorn, and Marvel movies, everything else is easy."

"Those are important," she said, biting off the top of the popsicle.

"Right?"

When she finished, she nursed the water for a little while and he got her phone so she could call the hospital and let them know she wouldn't be able to come in for her evening shift. "Okay, I'll see you on Saturday. Sorry, again, for the last-minute change," she said before hanging up.

Sean couldn't help but wonder why she had basically the whole week off. "Saturday? You have some vacation plans or something?"

"Oh, uh..." Looking down at her phone, she shook her head. "No, I, uh, just took some time off." She gave him a smile that felt forced. "I guess it's a good thing given how I feel."

"Yeah, well, let's get you back on your feet so you can enjoy at least some of your down time. You don't wanna miss Noah and Kristina's shindig on Friday night. His dad makes great burgers and Mo's bringing his ribs."

"Oh, Mo makes great ribs," she said.

"Yes, he does." Just thinking about them made Sean's belly growl. Man could not survive on popsicle alone.

She chuckled. "You better go take care of that. And I think I'll rest a while if that's okay."

"More than okay, D," he said. "What do you need before I go?"

Curling back on her side, she held up the washcloth. "Can you make this cold again?"

"Consider it done," he said. When he came back, she was taking her temp. "How's it looking?"

"One-oh-one-point-three now." She draped the cloth on her forehead, temple, and ear.

"Heading in the right direction at least," he said, really fuckin' glad she was doing a little better.

"Yeah, thanks for all this." Giving him a little smile, Dani tapped the edge of the cookie sheet.

"My cookie sheet of provisions is your cookie sheet of provisions," he said, wanting to give her a whole lot more.

Wanting to give her everything.

CHAPTER EIGHTEEN

DANI SLEPT on and off for two whole days. Between the fever, the nausea, and the headaches, she rarely got out of Sean's bed. But he was right there whenever she needed him. Not just with food or medicine, but with companionship. Making her smile and laugh. Anticipating her needs. Telling her stories. He even brought his laptop up so they could continue their Marvel marathon laying side by side in his bed during those windows when she was well enough to stay awake for a while.

With every passing hour, something became more and more clear to her—Dani was falling for him. As if he hadn't already gotten to her by covering her with a blanket and loving grilled cheese and tomato soup, he'd brought her every possible flu remedy on a cookie sheet and even brought her a spoon to go with the ice. And he'd held her hair while she threw up. Couldn't forget that.

She'd worried that good-guy Sean Riddick would be a problem, and she'd been right.

And then there was the way he'd been looking at her.

For days now, the cast of his eyes was both deeply concerned and fiercely protective. But there was something else there, too. Something that looked like longing. All of which Dani recognized because she was feeling the same way. With all of it. Concerned about the way his upbringing had twisted him up inside. Feeling protective of him—whether those attacks came from someone else or himself. And, oh, man, the longing. It resonated down deep.

Parts of her wanted Sean Riddick so damn bad, but then there were other parts that hesitated, cautioned, and even wanted to run away. It should've been easy. Boy likes girl. Girl likes boy. What was the problem?

Except Dani had built six years' worth of walls against exactly that kind of longing—walls meant to keep her from having to face the loss of a vital love ever again.

And now that her body wasn't so consumed by whatever virus had just run her butt over, her mind was starting to spin on the fact that tomorrow was the anniversary of Anthony's death. No way could she spend it with another man.

Which was why she pulled herself out of bed and dragged said butt into the shower. Being clean felt glorious after being so sick even though the simple act of showering took almost every ounce of her energy. So worth it.

Now came the problem of clean clothes. With a towel wrapped around her, she stepped out into Sean's bedroom and debated, and then opened a few drawers until she found what she needed—a pair of black boxers and a too-long T-shirt she knotted at her hip. She didn't feel too bad about rummaging through his things when he'd invited her just yesterday to help herself to whatever she needed.

"My clothes are your clothes." The memory made her smile. As so much about Sean Riddick did these days.

She was almost surprised he hadn't come upstairs when she heard his voice from downstairs. As she'd been just about to go down, she went out to the bannister to listen for a moment in case he had company, in which case she'd hide out here until they were gone. She was already worried enough that Sean was gonna get sick from how much time they'd spent together; she didn't want to infect somebody else.

It only took her a few minutes to realize he was on the phone. He seemed to be pacing between the dining room and the kitchen as he spoke, as his voice kept sounding louder and then softer and then louder again.

And then she heard him say something that made her stop in her tracks.

"...I know it sounds kinda corny, but I grew up watching Mr. Rogers, and him saying to look for the helpers when things are scary left a big impression on me. It's part of the reason I became a firefighter and went into the military. I wanted to be that for other people." There was a long pause, and then he continued, "Well, I'm really excited to be considered, to be honest with you. I think I'd get as much out of this as I hope a kid would hanging out with me." Another pause. "Okay, tomorrow at eleven works."

When he signed off, Dani dashed back into his room. She hadn't meant to eavesdrop, but it was just that she could hardly believe she'd just heard Sean Riddick reference Mr. Rogers. Not because there was anything wrong with that, of course, but because that was something her granny had said to her—beginning on that day twenty-six years ago when her father died.

Granny, are you trying to tell me something? Dani jokingly thought to herself.

And, hand to God, Granny answered, *"Live where you fear to live, Dani. That's where you'll find true joy."*

Dani heard Granny's voice plain as day. She would've sworn she did. Stunned, Dani sat heavily on the edge of the bed and pressed a hand to her forehead. The fever had broken, so she couldn't blame delirium for what she'd just heard—words she'd long forgotten her granny saying to her maybe a few months before she'd died. Dani had already become set on joining the military, and Nana didn't love the idea. Dani had gone to Granny to share that she was afraid Nana would be mad at and disappointed in her if she didn't drop the idea, and Granny had sat her down.

"Pay attention to the things that scare you, Dani. They're important. Sometimes they scare you because they're a true threat, but sometimes they scare you because they're the things you want and need so much you know it'll hurt if you don't get them. In those instances, live where you fear to live, Dani. That's where you'll find true joy. Little in life is worse than regret that you weren't brave enough to go after what you wanted."

It'd been classic Granny, and it had made Dani brave enough to sit down with Nana and Pap and tell them why the army was so important to her—not just because affording college otherwise would be tough for them, but also because she *wanted* to be a warrior. Just like the men she'd seen honored at the Black Leggings Warrior Society Ceremonial. It felt like it was part of her roots.

She'd won them over. She'd faced her fear about talking to them and not only were they *not* mad, but she'd earned their approval.

How had Dani forgotten that advice?

And why was she hearing it now?

The reason came walking into the room, all six-foot-two-inches of him, looking hot as usual in a pair of jeans and a worn black T-shirt.

"Hey, whoa, look at you. Showered and dressed. You're cookin' with gas," Sean said, grinning at her.

"Uh, yeah. I feel slightly more human today," she managed, her head still whirling a little bit as she struggled to make sense of the feeling that something really, really important had just happened.

"You okay?" Sean asked, crouching in front of her. He rested his big hands on her thighs.

"I think so. I just had the weirdest thing happen," she said, twisting the ring on her finger. "I thought I heard my grandmother's voice."

"Your granny's or your nana's?"

She blinked. At the fact that he was just accepting what she'd said at face value. And at the fact that he'd listened so carefully to her stories that he knew what she called her grandmothers. "It was Granny's voice." She waved a hand. "I mean, I'm sure it was just a really pronounced memory. Or déjà vu or something."

"Or maybe it was really her," Sean said, shrugging one big shoulder. "What did she say?"

"Wait, you really believe that?" Dani asked.

"I mean, maybe? Firefighters can be superstitious types and more than a few of the guys I know believe in ghosts, so..." He shrugged again. "Why not?"

His open-mindedness made him even sexier. "Wow, okay, well, she told me to live where I fear to live, which was something she said to me a long time ago."

"Do the thing that scares you," he said.

"Basically, yeah." She looked into his dark eyes and saw nothing but understanding and acceptance, and it made him feel like such a kindred spirit. Damn if all of this didn't give her something else to think about.

For the record, Granny, I heard you.

But she wasn't ready to take her grandmother's advice. Not yet. Not where Sean was concerned. So before he potentially asked what scared her, she blurted, "Hey, by the way, who were you talking to?"

DANI'S QUESTION caught Sean off guard not only because it felt like an abrupt change of subject but also because he hadn't realized she'd heard him on the phone.

"I mean, if you don't mind my asking. I wasn't trying to listen in, I was just making sure you didn't have company before I came downstairs."

"Oh." He smiled and ducked his chin. Shit, he was busted. Welp. Here went nothing. "Uh, it was an interview."

She gave him a funny look, clearly picking up on his sheepishness. "For what?"

After everything else he'd told her, this seemed like such a small thing to keep secret, even though he was going to feel like shit if they turned him down. So he laid it all out there. "Um, well, I applied to be a Big Brother." He shifted to sit on the bed beside her.

Dani frowned, and for a split second, his gut dropped to the ground thinking she disapproved. But then her eyes went wide and so did her smile. "Wait, what? Sean, this is awesome." God she was beautiful, sitting there wearing his clothes, her hair up in a sleek ponytail, looking at him like she believed in him.

Satisfaction filled his gut, but he shrugged it off and played it down. "I mean, they haven't approved me yet. They're coming to do a home inspection tomorrow." Which had him making a list of things he should think about doing around here before that happened. His grass needed cut. The spring on his front storm door needed repaired. But most importantly, he wanted to spiff up his currently super basic guest bedroom in case his Little ever just needed a place to crash or just hang out alone. Another safe place in the world that he could call his own. Something Sean never had.

Dani grinned. "Sean, they are totally going to approve you.

Your house is gorgeous and your basement would be any kid's dream. You have a good and very cool job. And you're a role model who's fun to hang out with. You're a shoe-in."

A role model? Wow. There she went again. Making him fall in love with her just a little bit more. "Yeah? You really think so?"

Facing him, she laced her hand into his. "I know it. This is so cool. Did Billy and Shayna get you into it?"

"Billy's stories about hanging out with his Little, Dante, just sounded like something I'd enjoy doing. I guess the accident has also left me feeling like there should be more to life than just work, you know? I mean, there's WFC, of course, and all of my friends there. But this is something that gives back, too." Of course, what he didn't say was how she fit into all that for him, because he really fuckin' wanted her to.

Dani kissed him, once, twice. "You're going to be a great Big Brother. I'm proud of you."

Fuck if that didn't put a knot in his throat. "Thanks, D," he managed, surprised at just how much those words meant to him. Coming from her, they meant a lot.

Do the thing that scares you.

Putting himself out there to become a Big Brother did scare him, but he realized that had nothing on the thing that truly scared him the most. And in that moment, Sean knew exactly what that was, because words were right on the tip of his tongue. Words he'd never said to anyone in his entire life.

He searched her gaze for a long minute and then just dove in, "Daniela, I—"

"Sean, I—" she said at the same time.

They both laughed.

Heart pounding in his chest, he nodded at her. "Go ahead, you first."

"Oh, okay. I was just going to say thank you for taking such good care of me the past few days. It's been a long time since I had anyone to do that for me."

"I was happy to do it, D," he said, sounding way more nonchalant than he actually felt.

She sat back, and he had the weirdest sensation that she was pulling away, but maybe that was just him freaking out over trying to tell her how he felt. "So...I think I'm gonna head out," she said. "I haven't been home since early Saturday morning and I have a few things I need to do and check on."

"Oh. Okay. Sure." Now he was pretty sure he'd read her right, which had him reining in his mouth.

"What were you going to say?" she asked, but there was a guardedness about her gaze that told him now was not the time.

So he gave her part of his truth. "Just that I've never shared everything I told you with anyone else, and I really appreciated how you supported me. It meant a lot."

There was warmth in the smile she gave him, and when she leaned close and kissed him, there was heat in the way she touched him. Those were reassuring, at least. "I feel the same way," she said.

All he could think was, *Do you, Dani? Because I feel it all, with you.* But what he said was, "I'll walk you out."

Fifteen minutes later, his phone beeped an incoming text, and it was her. *I'm home. Thanks again, Sean.*

Anything you need, Dani. Any time. Always.

She didn't reply, and it didn't exactly surprise him given that he had the distinct feeling that something had spooked her. Maybe it had something to do with what she'd thought she heard her granny say. Or maybe it had to do with him. So he didn't push her any further than that.

For now.

What *did* surprise him was that she didn't respond to his texts for the rest of the day. Not when he asked her opinion on two comforter sets he was considering at Target for the guest bedroom. Not when he texted her a photo of his freezer newly stocked with popsicles. And not when he sent her a 'Deadpool' meme that read, "If your left leg is Thanksgiving and your right leg is Christmas, can I visit you between the holidays?"

But most surprising of all was that she didn't respond when he texted her after the home inspection the next day.

It went fuckin' fantastic. The man who came was laid back and outgoing and totally put Sean at ease. The guy loved Sean's basement and thought kids would flip out to get to spend time there. He didn't see any problems and thought they'd be in touch with him next week given that tomorrow was the 4th.

He thought for sure Dani would respond to that news.

When she didn't, he called her...and got her voicemail.

Sean had no idea how to read any of that, but what he did know was that something felt very, very wrong. And he wasn't sure what to do about it.

CHAPTER NINETEEN

DANI HAD BEEN SITTING on her living room couch since midnight the night before. She was halfway through the sixth anniversary of Anthony's death.

Her comfiest blanket piled on her lap, Dani had spent a lot of that last thirteen hours staring at an envelope—the envelope that contained Anthony's just-in-case letter.

They'd both written one. Neither had ever expected for theirs to be read. Hers never had because she'd survived. But his hadn't been read either—because Dani had felt so guilty for not being at Anthony's side, for not even knowing he'd died until hours later, that she hadn't felt entitled to whatever comfort his last words to her might've offered.

Survivor's guilt was a bitch.

It got its talons deep into your skull and whispered all kinds of insidious little lies into your heart.

If you hadn't insisted on doing aeromedical evac, you might've been there for him when it mattered most.

He would be disappointed in you for not being brave enough to face what he had to say.

It should've been you.

Every year, she'd revisited those feelings, and found them still present in her mind and her heart. Sometimes they got quiet enough that she thought maybe they were finally gone, but July 3rd always came around to prove that they were still very much there.

Which was why, six years later, she still had the envelope. Worn now from her handling it year after year. One piece of the back unsealed from when she'd almost worked up the courage to open it last year.

"I'm sorry I haven't been braver, Anthony," she whispered, tears forming a knot in her throat.

From where her cell was charging in her bedroom, she heard another incoming text message. She'd finally moved it to the charger in there instead of keeping it within hand's reach out here on the couch—because Sean had been texting her on and off. And she'd just needed the space to work through all of this without being tempted to chat with him or laugh at his jokes or confront the fact that Dani had way stronger-than-friendly feelings towards him.

How strong was the part she couldn't deal with just then.

It didn't help that Dani still wasn't feeling good. No more fever or vomiting, fortunately, but she was still headachy and sometimes nauseous, and she hadn't eaten since the night before which probably wasn't helping since it was well after lunchtime.

Yeah. I should probably eat, she thought, staying right where she was, her brain half on autopilot whether or not her body needed fuel. She smoothed her hand over the plain white enve-lope. The only thing on the outside was her name in Anthony's slanted handwriting. She imagined that she could feel his touch through the envelope, through something he'd once touched. It was such a nice thought. But when her mind attempted to conjure up what that touch would feel like, it was *Sean's* much-bigger hand that she felt against her thighs, her wrists, her shoulders. It was Sean's touch, still fresh from all the time they'd just spent together, that now had the power to set her senses afire.

She burst into tears. Hugging the envelope to her chest, she sobbed. "I'm sorry, I'm sorry, I'm sorry."

This had happened before on this day. But in her heart of hearts, Dani suspected something was different. Part of her might've still been apologizing for not opening his letter. Part of her might've still been apologizing for getting to live while Anthony didn't. The tears came harder until her throat was so strained she barely made any noise at all. She just rocked herself with a shaking hand to her mouth, while tears streamed down her face.

Because this year, if she was being honest with herself, she *knew* something was different.

Part of her was also apologizing...for falling in love with another man.

And as much as that was a beginning, it was also an ending —an ending that meant it was finally time to let Anthony go.

Dani cried so hard and for so long that she crumpled over until she was lying in a ball against one arm rest, tears finally drained along with every bit of her energy. Blessedly, she fell asleep.

Knock, knock, knock.

She startled awake and had no idea what day or time it was. The blackness on the other side of her windows told her she'd been asleep for hours.

Knock, knock, knock.

"I'm coming," she tried to call, but her voice was little more than a froggy croak.

She untangled herself from the blanket and tossed it aside,

and then she stumbled to the door in the darkness. She had just enough presence of mind to peer through the peephole—and it was Sean she found standing on the other side.

Still disoriented, Dani opened the door. "Sean?"

His gaze did a complete once-over of her, making her realize she had no recollection of what she was even wearing. She looked down at herself—oh, right. An old gray army T-shirt that just barely covered her underwear...and nothing else.

She raked a hand through the rat's nest of her hair. "Uh, come in," she said, leaving him standing in the doorway as she retreated into her apartment and turned on the lamp next to the couch. She grimaced at the stack of used tissue that littered the coffee table. A few had tumbled to the carpet. But as he was already surveying the scene, it didn't make a lot of sense to try to hide the evidence of her sob-fest now. "Sit down if you like," she said, increasingly aware that he hadn't said a word yet. "Let me just, uh..." She thumbed over her shoulder. "Just gimme a minute."

He nodded. "Take your time, D."

She gave him a look long enough to take in just how freaking hot he was, even wearing just a pair of cargo shorts and a plain white T-shirt that highlighted the bulk of his shoulders and the muscle of his thighs. And did that man ever give good forearm. But she really didn't want to be thinking about Sean Riddick's hotness. Or his arm porn. Not today of all damn days.

Dani closed herself inside her bedroom and heaved a deep breath. She pulled on a pair of sleep shorts and then grabbed her phone off the nightstand. In the adjoining bathroom, she flicked on the light and made a face at her own reflection. Because the way she looked right now had to be in the dictionary next to "hot mess". Jesus. Her eyes were puffy and her skin was blotchy and her hair was all over the place.

She brushed her hair and teeth and held several handfuls of cold water against her eyes, but there was really no help for the bags hanging under them. For the time being, this was as good as she was gonna get.

Taking one last moment to collect herself, Dani woke up her phone to check her messages. The lock screen read:

12:04 AM
FRIDAY, JULY 4

She gasped. The anniversary was over. Competing reactions coursed through her. First, that she'd survived this day she so dreaded for another year. Second, that she felt less awkward having Sean here—and ogling all his hot-as-fuckness—now that it wasn't the anniversary. And, third...well, fuck.

Third was that Dani felt a little disappointed in herself for not opening Anthony's letter.

It was time. She wouldn't even beat herself up by saying it was *long past* time. Grief wasn't a state, it was a process. For better or worse, all of this had been her process. And it was a process that ultimately led to her being able to fall in love again, something she'd thought—no, *insisted*—she'd never again do. Even though the prospect of loving someone remained kinda freaking terrifying, it was Sean. Somehow he'd gotten behind or over her walls and made it so that loving him just felt...right.

The thought made her lean against the counter. Holy crap, she was in love. In love with the sexiest, bravest, funniest, snarkiest, dorkiest, most infuriating and most caring man she knew.

Live where you fear to live, Dani.

Now she knew why she was just remembering her granny's words after so very long. There were two things she'd most feared for all these years. First, reading Anthony's words. And second, the possibility of falling in love again—and of losing that love. And both of those fears were waiting to be faced on the other side of her bedroom door.

It didn't matter that the anniversary was over. It was time to read Anthony's letter. More than that, she couldn't wait to see what he'd written. But first there was Sean.

Taking a deep breath, she opened her bedroom door and went back out to the living room. She found Sean sitting on the couch. He looked up at her, eyes wide, head shaking. "I didn't mean it," he said.

Her gaze flashed down to his hand, to Anthony's envelope, which was torn open, the lined paper inside partly sticking out. She could hardly believe what she was seeing. She'd waited literal *years* to open this letter, and here he'd gone and done it. Rage absolutely roared through her. "What the fuck do you think you're doing?" she said, swiping it from his hand. "This was private. You had no fucking right."

Sean rose, palms raised. "I didn't mean to, Dani. I swear. I'm sorry."

"I can't believe you. You come over here uninvited in the middle of the night and...and what?" she sputtered. "You just thought you'd read something addressed to someone else?"

"Dani, I—"

"I barely know what to say to you right now, Riddick!"

He stepped closer and reached out for her. "Daniela—"

Dani reared back. "No," she said, backing away even further. "You have no idea what you've done. You just came Kool-Aid-man-ing into my life, and—" Shaking her head, she said, "You know what? I can't do this right now. My brain is literally on fire I'm so angry at you. I need you to go."

His expression went stony, and he gave a single nod. "If that's what you want."

She crossed her arms, trying to hold herself together. "It is."

Another nod. He made for the door. It seemed odd that someone so big could move so quietly, but he didn't make a sound until he put his hand on the doorknob. "For the record," he said in a low, rough voice. "I didn't read it."

"O-okay," she whispered, swiping at a single tear suddenly spilling from the corner of her eye.

He left.

And Dani was alone. Alone this time of her own making.

She felt like shit before he'd even fully closed the door, but she was so raw that she didn't know what to do.

Live where you fear to live, Dani.

One fear she held in her hand. The other was walking down the hall outside of her apartment. She looked down at the letter and saw the slant of Anthony's handwriting on the ruled pieces of loose-leaf paper.

She'd possibly never felt more torn in her whole life.

Dani bolted to the door. Wrenched it open. Stepped out into the hall. Sean was already gone. A rock dropped into her gut. She debated calling him to come back, but maybe this was fate saying to finish one book before she started another.

So even though the pull to go after Sean remained, she returned to the couch, sat with her legs tucked under her, and slid the letter out of the ruined envelope. Unfolding it made her heart trip into a sprint, and then all there was to do was read it.

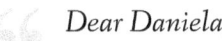

Dear Daniela,

Just in case I don't make it, I want you to know that you were everything I wanted and everything I could've ever asked for in a wife, a best friend, and a partner. I can't believe that I was lucky enough to turn your head in the first place—that was pretty near to a damn miracle. I can still picture you that very first time I ever saw you. Black hair shining in the sun while you were laying on a blanket in the Commons reading a book. I walked past three times until you finally looked up and I got your attention. I thought I'd been all stealthy about it and then you were like, how many more times are you going to circle by before you say hello? Do you remember that? That I've gotten to spend the last eight years with you, both of us sharing so many of the same passions and ideals, that's just been a dream, Daniela.

I want you to know that I am so proud of you. And if you ever need proof of that, just ask my guys how often I talk about you! I don't even have to, of course, because they all know your bad-ass reputation. But if you have any lingering worries about how I feel about your MEDEVAC work, put them aside now. Of course I worry. I can't stop that because I love you. But, Daniela, I see it. You were made to do that work. And I get to stand back and say, that bad-ass woman is mine.

Since you're reading this letter, that means I've left you. I'm so damn sorry for that. I know how many times you've been left and how many times you've had to deal with the pain of loss. I'm sorry I've brought you back to that place again. But know I would never have chosen to leave of my own free will. Right by your side was always where I was meant to be. It was the only place I ever wanted to be. Because you made my life happy. Full. Complete. God, we laughed and had fun, didn't we, Daniela? Thank you so much for that.

Now here's the part I really need you to hear: Live. And don't do it for me. Live for yourself. And don't just survive, but really live. Live and love and <u>*be happy.*</u> *That's what I want for you. Don't waste a single moment thinking I wouldn't want you to have a life full of love and family and kids and happiness. It's all I want for you. And if I can't be the one to give that to you, find someone who can and make sure he realizes what a lucky son of a bitch he is to have turned your head.*

So I guess that's what I want to say. I hope you never have to read this and that we get to grow old and gray together. But if that's not the way the chips fall, then know I loved you to the very end and beyond.

—Anthony

The second Daniela finished reading the letter, she started it again. And then she read it a third time, and a fourth. Her eyes were leaking whether she wanted them to or not, damnit, but she was also doing something that seemed so freaking impossible—she was smiling and laughing. She could hear Anthony's voice for the first time in *years*. It was like he was sitting there talking to her. She could see his crooked smile and the way he arched one eyebrow when he was calling her out on her shit.

Oh, God, why had she denied herself this letter—this healing, freeing, reassuring, *life-giving* letter—for so long?

An incredible lightness filled her chest, one that made it easier to breathe, one that lifted the weight she'd been carrying all these years. It felt nearly euphoric.

And now that she had finally read it, she wasn't going to waste a single minute before taking Anthony's advice.

She picked up her cell phone and called Sean. Without even ringing, it went directly to voicemail.

So she texted. *Hey. I'm sorry I freaked out. Can we please talk?*

Five minutes passed. Ten. That wasn't like him.

She didn't even debate it. She found a pair of flip flops, grabbed her purse and keys, and headed down to the garage. Worry was seeping around the euphoria. Worry that she'd really hurt Sean's feelings. Worry that she'd pushed him away. Worry that she'd blamed him for something he hadn't done, which was really the worst possible thing she could do to Sean.

Fuck. She'd fucked up. Especially because, even if he had opened the letter, in the end it'd given her a big push towards reading it. And she couldn't find anything to regret about having done that.

Everything appeared dark when she drove past the front of his house on 13ᵗʰ Street, but his bedroom and basement family room weren't visible from the front anyway. And maybe he'd already gone to sleep. In which case she wasn't sure what she was going to do.

But it turned out that didn't matter, because when she pulled into his backyard, his truck wasn't there.

Where the hell could he be at one-thirty in the morning?

Just to be sure, she killed the engine and walked up to the back door. The porch light wasn't on and she couldn't make out any light inside. Dani knocked. Waited. Knocked again a little harder. Standing there, she tried calling him again. But no luck. It still went straight to voicemail.

Dani's belly dropped to the floor.

And it pretty much stayed there for the next eighteen hours as she left voicemails and sent texts to which he didn't respond. She guessed that sorta served her right after she hadn't returned his texts or phone calls the day before. The thing was though, she hadn't done that on purpose, really. She'd done it because she'd been emotionally wrecked. And now her bones were telling her that he was doing it for the same damn reason.

With that feeling of dread rolling around in her gut, she got ready for Noah and Kristina's July 4th party. The last few days had been so messed up for her that she hadn't gotten around to making the pasta salad she'd volunteered to make, so she stopped by the fancy market with the great salads and bought some instead. And then, even though she was now officially running late, she drove by his house before she headed out of D.C. to Alexandria. His truck still wasn't there.

Should she just go to the party and assume he'd be there?

That didn't feel right.

Unsure what else to do, she called Billy.

"No, I haven't heard from him," Billy said. "Everything okay?"

"Uh, yeah," she said, probably not convincingly. "I was just trying to see if he wanted a ride out to Noah's."

"Sorry I couldn't help," Billy said. "We're almost there. Shayna says she can't wait to see you."

"Same here," she said, and then they hung up.

Staring at the back of his house, she debated, then dialed Mo.

"Hey, Mo, it's Dani."

"Hey, Dani," he said. "It's good to hear from you."

There was something in his voice, and she just knew. "He's with you."

"Yeah. And he's not in a good way." His words filled her with both relief and sadness. "You know why that is?"

"Yes," she said.

"I see." His tone communicated a whole lot more. Like, that he knew she had something to do with Sean's demeanor.

"Where are you?" she asked.

"We're at Noah's. You gonna come fix whatever this is?"

She was already backing out of Sean's yard. "I'm gonna try, Moses."

No, she was going to do more than that. She was going to explain herself. She was going to tell him how she really felt. She was going to fight for Sean Riddick with everything that she had.

CHAPTER TWENTY

SEAN WAS SHIT FOR COMPANY, and that was a massive fuckin' understatement. But Mo had dragged his ass to this party, which Sean had only gone along with since the guy had put up with Sean crashing at his place in the middle of the night without really telling him why.

Now Sean was sitting in a lawn chair surrounded by his friends who were all laughing and talking and trying to pretend like they couldn't tell he was absofuckin'lutely wrecked. At least nobody was asking him what was wrong. He wasn't sure he'd be able to say even if they did.

Because, Jesus, he couldn't get the devastated look on Dani's face out of his head. His gut was a noxious mess because of it. And his brain was right back to that old place. *You always, always hurt the people you care about, Riddick. This time, you messed up spectacularly and hurt the woman you love. And now you may never get to tell her that you love her in the first place.*

He really hadn't meant to open that damn letter.

He'd been nervously wandering her living room, looking at her pictures. He'd been to her place a few times before for different WFC get-togethers, but he hadn't ever paid too close attention to her pictures. Now, though, he knew who these people were. There was a picture of Dani in a cap and gown with an older couple who were probably her father's parents. There was young Dani with a man who she strongly resembled. He had to be her dad. There was another with her as a teenager at what looked like some kind of festival with an older lady who he guessed was Granny. And then there was one of her and a good-looking guy, both of them in army uniforms. Sean leaned in for a closer look. Both of them had the name 'England' on their patches. Her husband.

That was when he'd planted his ass on the couch. Because he felt like maybe he was snooping and he didn't want to upset her, especially given the way she'd looked when he got there—like a shell of her normal self. He'd already been worried out of his mind about her, if he were being honest, and then he'd arrived to find that she'd obviously been crying. Just as he feared, something had been really wrong, and he'd been kicking himself for not just coming over sooner.

All that was going through his head when he'd realized he was sitting on something. And when he pulled the envelope out from under himself, it caught on the button of the back pocket of his cargo shorts and ripped all the hell open.

At first, he wasn't sure what it was, and then the page inside the envelope shifted out enough for Sean to make out a few words: *I hope you never have to read this and that we get to grow old and gray together. But if that's not the way the chips fall, then know I loved you to the very end and beyond. —Anthony*

Nauseating words, because he knew exactly what this letter was—the *last* letter. And he couldn't fucking believe he'd ruined it.

And then she'd accused him of reading it. Of barging into her life unwelcome.

She'd asked him to get out.

He hadn't been able to go home because his house was now too filled with memories of her. So he'd ended up at Mo's.

A hand fell on his shoulder, and Sean flinched.

"Sorry," Shayna said, concern plain on her face. She tucked a red curl behind her ear. "Can I get you something?"

He attempted a smile. "No, Shay. Thanks, though."

She leaned down and planted a kiss on his cheek, and then she squeezed his shoulder and moved on without making a fuss that drew more attention his way. He really appreciated that.

He tried to at least appear interested in the conversation around him. Mo and Billy showed off the tattoos of griffins they both got to celebrate their new security firm, and Tara was entertaining everyone with her scarily encyclopedic knowledge of trivia, in this instance, about the real creature that mythological griffins were based on.

And that was when Sean saw Daniela come out the back door of the Cortez's house. Wearing a little black dress that looked kinda like a long T-shirt and those black Converse and dark sunglasses, her hair sleeked back in a ponytail. God, she was sexy and gorgeous and—really fuckin' angry at him.

She stood on the back deck and surveyed the party-goers, a mix of Noah's WFC friends and his parents' friends and neighbors, and Sean knew it the instant her gaze landed on him. Not just because she started heading his way, but because he felt it. Whatever that magnetism was between them remained despite the fact that he'd royally fucked up.

Dani said quick hellos as people noticed and stopped her, but she didn't linger in any of those conversations. She just kept moving in his direction, and he had no clue exactly what was coming at him—nor was he sure he wanted to find out in front of all these fine people.

No superhero here, and all that.

So he got up and started threading around the outside of

their group, and still she made for him. And then she was right there in front of him. "Can we talk?"

He hesitated.

She lifted her sunglasses on top of her head. Her eyes weren't swollen and red like they'd been last night, but that wasn't to say that she looked good exactly. She still looked upset, which made that boulder in his gut even heavier. "Please?"

"Uh, I don't know, Dani," he said, moving away from the group. Not really wanting everyone to hear what a shitty thing he'd done. Not wanting her to hand him his ass at this particular moment after he'd been doing such a stellar job kicking it himself. "Now's probably not the best time."

"When, then? I've been calling and texting."

She had? He'd turned his phone off last night after he left her place and hadn't turned it back on again, figuring it wouldn't matter anyway. He frowned. "Yeah, sounds like me the day before."

Dani ducked her chin and nodded, and man if he didn't feel like an asshole. "I know," she said, "and I'm sorry."

"You don't have to apologize to me, Daniela. You don't owe me anything." Sean powered on his phone, surprised when a barrage of missed calls and message notifications popped up, but he swiped past those and thumbed on the ride app. It was going to cost him a fuck-ton of cash to get from where the Cortezes lived out here near Mount Vernon back into the city but leaving was for the best.

"Wait, what are you doing?" she asked.

"I'm gonna head out," he said, waiting for the frustratingly slow app to load. He walked a few paces away, hoping to pick up another bar and get a stronger signal.

"Stay," she said.

The word tugged at something inside his chest, even as the app finally loaded and he hit the button to request a pick-up.

Surprisingly, there was a car only five minutes away. He shook his head. "My ride's gonna be here in five. I gotta go say my good-byes."

He went to the picnic table where most of the WFC gang—Mo, Billy, Shayna, Noah, Kristina, Jud, Jesse, and Tara—were all laughing at some story that Jud was telling, his southern drawl loud and animated. Sean braced his hands on Mo's big shoulders. "I'm sorry to say this, but I'm gonna go. I'm not... feeling great."

As everyone called out their regrets and sympathies, Mo peered over his shoulder. "You sure you need to go?"

"Yeah, man."

Frowning, Mo nodded. "You need a ride?"

"No, you stay and enjoy. I'm covered." He gave everyone a wave, but when he turned to leave, Dani was standing just a few feet away. "See ya, D."

"Sean," she said, catching his arm with her hand.

"I don't want to fight, Dani."

"I don't want to fight, either," she said, following him.

"Then what do you want?" he asked, not stopping.

"I want you to stay and talk to me," she said, and he had to admit that there was something in the tone of her voice that tempted him to consider it. Because she sounded upset, but she didn't sound angry.

Even so, this still wasn't the place. He sighed. "My car's gonna be here in two minutes."

"Forget the car, Sean."

He rounded on her. "I'm trying not to barge in on your life here."

She nearly crashed into him and had to put a hand on his chest to catch herself. "I deserved that."

"Fuck, no you didn't, which is why I'm fuckin' leaving." He walked away, aware that they were attracting attention now.

"What if I don't want you to go?" she called as he reached the side of the house.

Not wanting to let anymore of his hurt spew out on her, he just waved a hand.

"Sean!"

He kept going.

"What if I fucking love you?" she yelled.

Sean froze. His heart was a sudden freight train in his chest. Slowly, he turned and nailed her with a stare. "What did you say?"

Her black eyes were glassy and filled with so much emotion. "I said I fucking love you, Sean Riddick."

He was a thousand per cent aware that the party had gone silent behind Dani, but all he could see was her. His pulse beat so hard he felt it against his skin and heard it in his ears. "Don't say something you don't mean, Daniela."

"I mean it." She hugged herself. "I love you, and I'm so sorry that I yelled at you. I said things I didn't mean and—"

He stalked toward her. Just walked right up and took her into his arms. "Say it again."

Her lower lip quivered. "I love you." He saw the truth of it in her eyes. Heard it in her voice.

It nearly took him to his knees. "Jesus Christ, Dani. I fuckin' love you, too." He kissed her then, and it was a kiss unlike any he'd ever had. It was filled with passion and heat—the stuff they'd always been good at. But in the way she touched his face and held fast to his shoulder, he felt claimed. No, more than that, he felt *wanted* for the first time in his whole damn life. When they finally broke apart, Sean shook his head. "The envelope ripped on my shorts, D. I swear to God I didn't try to read it."

Still holding him tight, she pressed a kiss to his lips. "It wasn't your fault. I shouldn't have taken out how I was feeling on you. I know it was really unfair. Yesterday...yesterday was the anniversary of my husband's death. It's always been a hard day for me, in part because I'd never opened his last letter—"

"Oh, Jesus, Dani. I'm so fuckin' sorry."

She cupped his cheek in her hand, and it was so sweet he couldn't resist pressing against her touch. "Stop, please," she said. "You couldn't have known any of this. I could've told you but I didn't because I was all up in my head about it. Confused because of how I was feeling about you when I'd convinced myself that I would never put myself out there this way again. I'd already decided I was going to read the letter, so you didn't do anything wrong."

"I don't want to hurt you. Not ever," he said, appreciating her honesty and reassurance.

"I don't ever want to hurt you, either. But here's the thing, we're gonna mess up sometimes, but if we promise to stay and talk it out, we'll get through it. You know?" she asked, smiling at him with what looked like hope in her eyes.

Damn, he felt that, too. "Yeah? I can do that. I'd do anything for you. Jesus," he said, resting his forehead against hers, "I can't believe you love me."

"Get used to it, Riddick, you're stuck with me."

His grin was immediate. "That's the best thing I've ever heard." He kissed her again, deep and slow and thoroughly.

And that was when the applause and cat calls started.

They broke apart to find their friends losing their ever-loving minds. Clapping and cheering and on their feet—Billy and Noah actually stood on top of one of the picnic tables. Shayna and Tara were hugging each other and batting away happy tears.

"It's about damn time," Mo called, raising a beer. That set off another round of pandemonium.

Daniela laughed. "I guess we should go join the party. I think the secret's out."

He smirked. "Ya think? Anyway, no dice. I want you all to myself. Wave good-bye."

"What?"

"Wave good-bye to all the nice people."

"What do you—"

Sean lifted her into a fireman's carry over his shoulder, then waved to his friends who were now laughing their asses off. Not that he minded one bit.

"Sean!" Dani yelled—though there was laughter in there, too. "Put me down!"

"Not a chance, D," he said, feeling better than he'd felt maybe ever. He couldn't believe what was happening but he wasn't wasting a minute questioning it. Not when he had everything he wanted right here in his arms.

"But what about the fireworks?" she said. "We should at least stay for the fireworks."

He guffawed. "Oh, there'll be fireworks, all right, Daniela. I guaranfuckin'tee it. You just tell me how many fireworks you want and I'll make sure you have them." An SUV was waiting in the driveway. Perfect timing.

As he approached it, Dani smacked his butt. "Geez, wait a sec. What about my car?"

Sean stopped in his tracks. "Oh. Oh, shit. I didn't think of that." He went up to the passenger window of the SUV and gestured for the guy to put down the window. "Hey, sorry man, my bad. I don't need the ride anymore, but...hang on."

"Oh, my God, put me down," Dani said, humor and murder plain in her voice.

He retrieved his wallet from his back pocket and pulled out a couple of twenties. "For your trouble." The driver laughed, thanked him, and pulled away.

"I can't believe you just talked to that dude while carrying me around like a damn caveman," Dani said.

Sean just laughed and carried her the rest of the way to her car, parked along the edge of the yard under the shade of some big trees. He put her down so that she sat on the car's hood near the driver's door, then stepped between her legs, his hands on her hips.

"Jesus, D, is this really happening?" he asked.

"Yeah, I think it is." She smiled, and she was so fuckin' pretty it stole his breath. How the hell had he gotten so lucky?

"We can stay and watch the fireworks if you want," he said.

She shook her head, her gaze suddenly full of heat. "I'd prefer your kinda fireworks."

"Is that right?"

She grinned and took his cheek in her hand. "Mmhmm. What's the line? 'This is a face I'd be happy to sit on'...?"

The 'Deadpool' reference made Sean throw back his head and laugh. But what really left a lasting impression on him about that moment was that she'd chosen a quote that had been all about Vanessa's unconditional acceptance and love of Deadpool, ugly-ass scars and all. And that was when, if he hadn't known it already, Sean became totally and completely sure that Daniela England was the only woman for him.

"Damn, I love you," he said, kissing her until she was fisting her hands in his shirt.

Panting, she said, "You realize it's gonna take forever in 4th of July traffic to get home."

"Shit, I hadn't thought of that."

"That's because all of your blood flow has traveled south." She palmed his hard-on.

"That's fuckin' true," he said, groaning at her touch.

He peered down toward the dead-end of the street on which the Cortezes lived. Her gaze followed his. That's where his truck had been parked for Noah's Halloween party, the first time they'd ever gotten together....

"Are you serious?" she asked.

"Are you game?" he challenged.

Like giddy, reckless teenagers, they moved the car to the mostly hidden dead end. Annnd that was how they ended up still being at Noah's house when the actual fireworks went off an hour later. Not that they could see them very well from Dani's tiny back seat. Neither of them complained.

They'd come full circle in a way that Sean could hardly believe. Somehow, he'd gotten knocked off of his ass and right into the arms of the best woman he'd ever known. What was between them was intense and powerful and brand new and red hot. But this was one fire that Sean Riddick had absolutely no intentions of fighting. Not now. Not ever.

CHAPTER TWENTY-ONE

THREE MONTHS LATER...

DANI FINISHED LOADING the last of her dinnerware into Sean's kitchen cabinets and tossed aside the empty boxes. Well, *their* kitchen cabinets now.

Just like everything else about their relationship, the weeks following Noah's party had been an absolute whirlwind, and by the end of the summer, Sean had invited her to move in. After years of putting up walls against all the things she wanted, Dani had been surprised to find that she was just as eager as Sean to wake up together every morning and go to bed together every night. Or, at least, the nights and mornings that one or the other of them didn't work—because Sean had gotten a clean bill of health on his eye and was back out there fighting fire. So Dani had given notice on her apartment and moved in as October brought a crispness to the fall air.

That'd been two weeks ago. Now, they were just about done figuring out how to blend all their furniture and possessions.

Dani left the basement exactly how Sean had it—because she loved it just the way it was. The rest had been pretty easy, too.

"You sure you don't mind me going out?" Sean asked as he swept into the kitchen wearing a pair of jeans and a DCFD sweatshirt and looking fine as hell, scars and all. "I know we have a few more things to go through."

"No," she said. "I think Tara and I might do something anyway, so go have fun."

He pinned her against the counter, braced his hands on either side of her hips, and waggled his eyebrows. "I know how we could have lots of fun."

Grinning, Dani rolled her eyes. "There'll be time for that later."

"Promise?" he asked.

She laughed. "Do I ever tease you about sex?"

"All the fuckin' time, woman," he said, kissing her soundly.

When they finally broke apart, she laced her arms around his neck. "What are you guys gonna do today?"

"Lunch at Ben's Chili Bowl and then shopping for a birthday gift for his little brother." Sean shrugged. "After that, I'm not sure. Whatever he wants is fine by me."

"That sounds nice," Dani said, loving how much Sean was enjoying being a Big Brother. The week after the 4th of July, he'd received his match with a ten-year-old boy named Tyson Marvin and they were thick as thieves already. Of course, it didn't hurt that the boy loved comic books and Sean basically had the sense of humor of a ten-year-old. Dani just adored how good Sean was with Tyson. The way he mentored and looked out for that boy made her love Sean Riddick even more.

When had she *ever* been able to resist good-guy Sean? Clearly the answer was never.

Sean kissed her cheek, then grabbed a bottle of water from

the fridge. "Maybe tonight if you're up to it we can begin our X-Men marathon."

She laughed. They'd finished the Marvels Avengers marathon during the summer. There'd been more than twenty movies! And she enjoyed the heck out of them all. "How many movies are in this universe?"

"Woman," he said, surprising her when he scooped her up and sat her on the counter. "Just go along for the ride here, would ya?"

She smirked. "Another robust universe?"

"Something like that." He planted a quick kiss on her lips. "Gotta go. I'll text you and let you know what time I'll be home."

"Sounds good," she said, appreciating the view as she watched him leave. Damn that man did all kinds of justice to a pair of jeans. Smiling, she sat right where he'd placed her for a long moment and thought about what he'd said.

Home.

That word didn't just sound good to her, it felt *true.*

She was home. For the first time in so long. Really, she felt that way whenever she was with Sean. That was her new truth.

Dani picked up her phone and texted Tara. *Hey, the boys are off playing so I am free for maid of honor duties all day long!*

Tara responded right away. *Oh, I am totally taking you up on that!*

Smiling as they made a plan, Dani realized how far she'd come these past few months. Her happiness for her friend was genuine and easy now. The pain she'd carried for so long was gone. It wasn't that she never missed Anthony, but it was different now. The happy memories had become comforting to remember. And she could talk about Anthony in a way she hadn't for years. It was like finding a part of herself again.

To that end, she'd emailed the Kiowa tribe's enrollment

office which kept records related to all its members to see if it had any genealogical information about Granny's family. These days, she was all about nurturing the roots of the life she'd become determined to have. One with love and family and connection and meaning. And happiness—just like Anthony had wished for her.

It was all due to Sean Riddick, her biggest champion, her fighter, her hero, her best friend.

The man who helped her find the strength to fight again.

After so long, Dani could truly and finally say she had everything she needed and so much that she wanted. Now, she was going to fill her days with love and laughter and make sure to appreciate the amazing ways her life had changed every damn day—to the very end and beyond.

THE WARRIOR FIGHT CLUB SERIES

Fighting for Everything

Loving her is the biggest fight of his life...

Home from the Marines, Noah Cortez has a secret he doesn't want his oldest friend, Kristina Moore, to know. It kills him to push her away, especially when he's noticing just how sexy and confident she's become in his absence. But, angry and full of fight, he's not the same man anymore either. Which is why Warrior Fight Club sounds so good.

Kristina loves teaching, but she wants more out of life. She wants Noah—the boy she's crushed on and waited for. Except Noah is all man now—in ways both oh so good and troubling, too. Still, she wants who he's become—every war-hardened inch. And when they finally stop fighting their attraction, it's everything Kristina never dared hope for.

But Noah is secretly spiraling, and when he lashes out, it threatens what he and Kristina have found. The brotherhood of the fight club helps him confront his demons, but only Noah can convince the woman he loves that he's finally ready to fight for everything.

Fighting for What's His

Resisting her only makes him want her more...

Private investigator Billy Parrish's is good at three things—fighting, investigating, and sex. MMA training with the other vets in the Warrior Fight Club keeps his war-borne demons at bay—mostly, and one night stands ensure no one gets too close. But then his best friend from the Army Rangers calls in a favor.

Shayna Curtis is new to town, fresh out of grad school, and full of hope for the future. With a new job starting in a month, she's grateful when her brother arranges a place for her to stay while she apartment hunts. But she never expected her roommate to be so brooding. Or so sexy.

Billy can't wait for Shay to leave—because the longer she's there, the more he wants her in his bed. To stay. He *can't* have her—that much he knows. But when fight club stops taking off the edge, Billy lets down his guard...and starts fighting for what's his.

Worth Fighting For

A crossover story with Kristen Proby's Big Sky Series

Getting in deep has never felt this good...

Commercial diving instructor Tara Hunter nearly lost everything in an accident that resulted in her medical discharge from the navy. With the help of the Warrior Fight Club, she's fought to overcome her fears and get back in the water where she's always felt most at home. At work, she's tough, serious, and doesn't tolerate distractions. Which is why finding her gorgeous one-night stand on her new dive team is such a problem.

Former navy deep-sea diver Jesse Anderson just can't seem

to stop making mistakes—the latest being the hot-as-hell night he'd spent with his new partner. This job is his second chance, and Jesse knows he shouldn't mix business with pleasure. But spending every day with Tara's smart mouth and sexy curves makes her so damn hard to resist.

Joining a wounded warrior MMA training program seems like the perfect way to blow off steam—until Jesse finds that Tara belongs, too. Now they're getting in deep and taking each other down day and night, and even though it breaks all the rules, their inescapable attraction might just be the only thing truly worth fighting for.

Fighting the Fire

One night is never enough…

For firefighter Sean Riddick, Warrior Fight Club keeps the demons of his past at bay, even though it means seeing Daniela England. Her ball-busting sarcasm drives him nuts, and he knows he's damaged goods anyway, but he can't help but remember how good they were together that one time. Now he wants to take her to the mats no matter how much they go toe to toe.

ER nurse Daniela England has lost so much that she's vowed never to need anyone again. Fight club helps her beat back her survivor's guilt, but it means dealing with Riddick. The hot-but-infuriating firefighter is everything she wants to avoid, which is why their one-night stand was a mistake. Now she needs to keep her distance so it doesn't happen again.

But when Dani witnesses Sean's motorcycle accident, she steps up to help him recover. One on one, they get beneath all the snark and find a connection neither expected. As Sean heals, the sparks between them burst into red-hot passion—and ignite old wounds. Now there are fires all around—and they have to decide which they'll fight and which they'll let consume them.

ACKNOWLEDGMENTS

This was the book that almost didn't happen.

If you follow me on social media, you might know some of the trials I went through while writing *Fighting the Fire*. I started writing it while injured and awaiting my first rotator cuff surgery and then got further delayed when, four weeks after that surgery, I fell and severely reinsured my shoulder. However, I didn't know that for sure at the time because my surgeon wanted to wait before getting a new MRI. So in the meantime I pushed through with physical therapy and trying to finish this book for its new release date. I forced myself to work hard through the pain for two weeks to make that date only for my laptop to be stolen the day that I'd written all but the last chapter. And then I learned that all my backups failed. Dropbox hadn't synched those last 120 pages I'd written during that final push. The back-up file on my Apple Time Machine at home was corrupted, and though the Mac Medics were able to recover the file, it didn't contain those new pages either.

I was crushed.

And I was too exhausted and in too much pain to be productive. Finally, a new MRI revealed the extent of the now massive rotator cuff tear I had (3 of the 4 rotator cuff tendons were torn, one in two places, and one of my biceps tendons was also torn) and a new surgery was scheduled, one that the surgeons gave only a 50% chance of being successful. That was really scary, because the options for what happened if the surgery failed were all bad.

The surgery was a success!

Well, mostly. On a good day, I probably have about 80% of my strength and function back. The BEST thing is that most of the time my shoulder is now pain free. And that is truly amazing. But it took all of the crazy year of 2020 to get to a place where I could really write again and to remove all the mental hurdles I'd put up around this book and these characters.

And I'm so damn glad I was able to do it. Because I adore Dani and Sean. I love their banter. I love that they're both bad asses *and* nerds. I love that they never imagined how much they had in common with each other, and I adored writing that discovery. I hope you love them, too.

There were a number of people who helped me get to the other side of all these misfortunes. My husband, Brian, and our daughters were so supportive and took such good care of me. My closest friends, Lea Nolan, Stephanie Dray, Christi Barth, and Kate Quinn were relentless cheerleaders who provided motivation and shoulders to cry on in equal measure. Robin Covington provided a much-needed and very appreciated sounding board at a critical juncture. I appreciated every time my assistant, Franci Neill, checked in on me and that she was always so excited for this book to be completed. Thank you to my agent, Kevan Lyon, who was a great advocate and was always so understanding. I must also give a special shout-out to the team at Audible who gave me the leeway I needed to get through this rough patch until I could deliver the book to them.

I'm so grateful that the amazing Andi Arndt was still able to narrate this book, too!

I also have to thank the readers in my Ravens Facebook group for all the support, love, and excitement they've shown me through this whole situation. I never received anything except understanding and compassion in response to the delays on this book and it truly has meant the world to me.

I hope you enjoyed this story. It meant so much to me to finally write it, and I thank you for taking my characters into your heart and letting them tell their stories again and again. ~LK

ABOUT THE AUTHOR

Laura Kaye is the New York Times and USA Today bestselling author of over forty books in contemporary romance and romantic suspense, including the Hard Ink, Raven Riders, Heroes, and Hearts in Darkness series. Her books have received numerous awards, including the RT Reviewers' Choice Award for Best Romantic Suspense for *Hard As You Can*. Laura grew up amid family lore involving angels, ghosts, and evil-eye curses, cementing her life-long fascination with storytelling and the supernatural. Laura lives in Maryland with her husband and two daughters, and appreciates her view of the Chesapeake Bay every day.

Learn more at LauraKayeAuthor.com

facebook.com/laurakayewrites

twitter.com/laurakayeauthor

instagram.com/laurakayeauthor

bookbub.com/profile/laura-kaye

www.ingramcontent.com/pod-product-compliance
Lightning Source LLC
Chambersburg PA
CBHW070104280626
47159CB00016B/1285